I staggered but he kept me upright, his face so close to mine that I could smell the fish on his breath. I stared into his battle-hardened face and the long red scar that puckered one corner of his mouth, and realized that this was the samurai who had crept along the corridor to my mother's chamber earlier. My hand gripped tighter on the hilt of my sword.

"I've been tracking you silly girls since you left the banqueting hall." He sneered. "And you never suspected a thing." He sniggered, a nasty, low, rasping sound, and tightened his grip on my throat.

I couldn't breathe. Blood pounded in my ears.

As he raised the point of his sword to my throat he whispered, "I will be well rewarded for killing you!"

MAYA SNOW

Sisters of the Sword

HARPERTROPHY®

AN IMPRINT OF HARPERCOLLINS*PUBLISHERS*

Sisters of the Sword
Copyright © 2008 by Working Partners Limited
Series created by Working Partners Limited
www.harpercollinschildrens.com

Library of Congress Cataloging-in-Publication Data
Snow, Maya.
　Sisters of the sword/ by Maya Snow. — 1st ed.
　　p.　cm.
　Summary: Two aristocratic sisters in ancient Japan disguise
themselves as samurai warriors to take revenge on the uncle
who betrayed their family.
　ISBN 978-0-06-124389-9
　[1. Samurai—Fiction. 2. Revenge—Fiction. 3. Disguise—
Fiction. 4. Sex role—Fiction. 5. Sisters—Fiction. 6. Japan—
History—1185–1600—Fiction.] I. Title.
PZ7. S685115Si 2008　　　　　　　　　　　2007029610
[E]—dc22　　　　　　　　　　　　　　　　　　　　CIP
　　　　　　　　　　　　　　　　　　　　　　　　　　　AC

Typography by Andrea Vandergrift
09 10 11 12 13 CG/CW 10 9 8 7 6 5 4 3 2 1
❖
First Harper Trophy edition, 2009

For Ellis and Claudia—
two inspirational young women

ACKNOWLEDGMENTS

Special thanks to Helen Hart

Thanks also to Dr. Phillip Harries
of The Queen's College, Oxford,
for his invaluable advice and expertise

Sisters of the Sword

PROLOGUE

I have become invisible.

Imagine you are making your way along a bustling street in the Imperial Capital of Heiankyo, rubbing shoulders with craftsmen and merchants. You push through the crowd, touching me, but you still do not see me.

Perhaps you are walking alone through a deserted alleyway in some remote village. You might walk right past me and never notice.

I can move as silently as a ghost. Unseen by the human eye. And when I strike, I strike fast. You could be dealt a deathly blow, and yet never see who or what had killed you.

But I would not draw my sword against you. Because to kill without reason, in cold blood, is against the *bushi*, the samurai code. And I am a samurai.

Ah, I see you blink with surprise. *A girl?* you are thinking. *Surely a girl cannot be a samurai!*

But you are wrong. My sister, Hana, and I have

1

proved that girls can be samurai. Together we have honored our father's memory by treading the path of the warrior, a path full of hardship, danger, and death.

It is strange to think that I once knew little of danger, and nothing of death.

But now, death stalks me. A dark shadow follows my every footstep, watches my every move. I can hide from you in the streets, but I cannot hide from death.

Oh yes. Death and I have come to know each other very well.

CHAPTER ONE

I was in the moss garden when the bell tolled to announce the approach of a visitor at the gate.

"Yamamoto no Hidehira!" The watchman cried Uncle's name from the watchtower. "*Ima tsukitamaisoro!*" He is arriving!

My heart jumped with excitement and I dropped the bamboo cane I'd been using as a practice sword. Two energetic leaps took me over the gravel beds and across the narrow stream that snaked through the moss garden.

"Kimi, slow down!" my mother called from a nearby pavilion. "Remember what your grandmother always used to say—"

"Yes, yes!" I called back. "The first daughter of his lordship, the *Jito,* should not behave like a farmworker!"

My mother laughed. "And are you behaving like a farmworker, Kimi?" she asked.

"Of course not," I replied, smiling.

To honor my grandmother's memory, I proceeded in a ladylike fashion all the way to the end of the path with my hands inside the wide sleeves of my silk robe. But being a lady all the time was too much for me. I would rather spend my days fighting and studying the *bushi* code, like my father and brothers do. So the moment I was out of sight of my mother's pavilion, I broke into a run and raced to the side courtyard.

I arrived at the entrance to the courtyard just in time to see Uncle Hidehira dismount from his horse. He was a big man, dark eyed and dark haired, dressed in robes of glossy red silk that befitted his important station as brother to the *Jito*. Plates of lacquered armor were strapped to his chest, arms, and legs, the iron panels laced together with strips of strong rawhide. I could see my uncle's favorite *tanto* dagger fastened tightly at his waist by a narrow silk sash. The bright red-lacquered decoration on its ornate scabbard glittered in the late-afternoon sun.

Surrounding Uncle Hidehira was his entourage of about thirty samurai soldiers in full armor, their faces stern beneath elaborate helmets. Long curving bows and quivers of arrows bristled at their backs as they leaped gracefully off their mounts and tossed the reins to a gaggle of waiting servants. I felt a thrill as I watched the samurai. They looked poised and

4

fierce in their hardened leather armor.

"One hour's rest for the men," my uncle said curtly to his captain. "Then I want the weapons made ready for inspection."

As his soldiers received their orders from the captain, Uncle turned to survey the compound that had been his childhood home. One hand rested casually on the hilt of his *tanto* dagger as his dark gaze settled on the red-painted pillars and graceful, curved rooftops of the pavilions. I saw him smile as he took in the beautiful gardens that went down in sweeping steps all the way to the green valley far below.

I stepped forward out of the shadow of the gateway and Uncle caught sight of me.

"Little Kimi!" he cried as he stretched out his hands toward me and came striding across the courtyard. "All dressed in silk robes with her long hair down her back. You've grown since I saw you last year. I suppose I shouldn't call you 'little' anymore. You're as tall as a willow tree and twice as strong." He clasped my hands in his and I was aware of his great strength. "Have you come running to see if I've brought presents for you?"

I laughed and shook my head. "Seeing you again is better than any present, Uncle." I glanced past him and surveyed the samurai, searching for a smaller figure among the men. "Is Ken-ichi with you?"

"Your cousin is in training," Uncle answered. "These days he has no time for visiting. He must focus on his studies if he is ever to be a worthy samurai." Uncle's eyes crinkled at the corners as he regarded me. "And how are your own studies, Kimi? Have you remembered the *kata* I taught you when I was here last year?"

"Yes, Uncle," I replied, bowing to show my gratitude for his teaching. "I practice the sword movements you showed me every day."

Training with a sword was not usually part of a noble lady's education, but Father insisted that all women in his household knew how to defend themselves and their home in case of an attack. He even indulged our training in men's weapons like the sword because, as he said, both Hana and I had shown exceptional talent. Tea ceremonies, dancing, and calligraphy were one thing, but it was weapons training and martial skills that thrilled me the most.

"I remember I was impressed with the way you handled a sword," Uncle said with a thoughtful nod. "You should have been born a boy, Kimi. What a warrior you would have made!"

I smiled as I led Uncle up the stone steps and along a covered walkway toward the entrance hall. *One day,* I thought, *I will show my family that even a girl can be a great warrior.*

"I've also been training with the *naginata* spear," I told him as we walked.

"An excellent defense weapon," Uncle said. "You'll need that if any rebels ever attack the compound. How many of the basic postures have you covered, Kimi?"

"All six," I said proudly. "And I can attack a target from above *and* below!" I swept my hand in a wide curve to show Uncle one of my moves.

As I told him about my training and what I had been reading about in my Zen studies, servants in loose cotton trousers and baggy blue jackets followed respectfully behind us, carrying Uncle's baggage. The samurai soldiers had disappeared off to their own quarters, no doubt to prepare for weapons inspection.

Up ahead, a slanting beam of sunlight captured my younger sister, Hana, as she emerged from the entrance hall. She was dressed in a thick, sea-green silk kimono that rippled like water as she moved toward us. My grandmother would never have called Hana a farmworker—she was always poised and elegant. Her name means "flower," and I often think of how well my parents named her. She is grace itself.

I gave a little wave and Hana answered with a smile, her gentle face full of welcome as she bowed to Uncle. Behind her scampered our youngest brother, Moriyasu, dressed in yellow with the bottom of his trousers still damp from playing in the pond. He gave a yelp of delight when he saw our visitor and waved his *bokken*, the little wooden sword that rarely left his hand.

Hana came to stand at my side, her fingers briefly touching mine in our secret signal of kinship. As Moriyasu dashed down the steps to Uncle, Hana and I stood side by side, giggling softly behind our hands as we watched our brother's antics.

"Hai-ya!" Moriyasu shrieked as he kicked up one foot and pretended to stab Uncle with a swift sword movement. "You're dead! I killed you!"

Uncle clutched his stomach, bending over as if he had been mortally wounded. "Aai!" he groaned. "An old man like me is no match for such a skilled young samurai!" He straightened up and lightly pinched Moriyasu's cheek. "Keep up your practice, young man, and perhaps one day the great Shogun himself, Minamoto no Sanetomo, will employ you as his bodyguard."

Moriyasu's eyes widened. "Do you think so, Uncle? What an honor that would be for our family! I would be like you then, serving the Shogun just as you serve my father."

Moriyasu's voice was full of admiration, but I held my breath for a moment. Would his innocent words offend Uncle? It was not polite to remind a strong

8

man like Hidehira that he must serve his younger brother.

But Uncle cheerfully ruffled Moriyasu's short black hair. "So you want to be like me, eh? Well, I think you have some growing to do first, little warrior!"

We all made our way toward the *shinden*, the elegant pavilion that was the center of our home. My mother came out to meet us, all the elegance of her station reflected in her beautiful pale face and dark eyes. Her smooth hair was worn loose to the waist like mine, and it shone like black silk as she bowed to Uncle.

"Welcome, Hidehira," she said softly. "As always, it is a pleasure to see you. My husband is in the rock garden with his secretary. Yoshijiro was finishing some paperwork while he waited for you to arrive."

"My brother works too hard," Uncle said with a smile.

"Perhaps," my mother replied, bowing respectfully. "But Yoshijiro always says that the *Jito*'s job is as much about proper administration as it is about fighting."

"Wise words," Uncle acknowledged politely. "The Shogun would approve."

My mother led him through the square rooms, where the paper walls seemed to whisper as we passed. Moriyasu danced at Uncle's heels, swinging his wooden sword.

Hana and I followed behind, falling into step together. As we walked, I felt calmness settle over me. My sister was the tranquil influence that soothed my restless energy.

We made our way out of the house and followed a line of cherry blossom trees to the rock garden. I could see my father sitting on a wooden bench in a patch of golden sunshine. His black hair was twisted into a knot on the top of his head, and his brow was creased in concentration as he held back his heavy, yellow silk sleeve and dipped his brush onto his wet inkstone. He made a series of quick, firm brush-strokes on a paper scroll, and then handed the scroll to his secretary who stood nearby.

My father was very wise and learned, and he worked from dawn until dusk in his role as *Jito*, Lord Steward, a representative of the Shogun himself. He presided over a large southern part of the Kai Province, but however hard he worked, he was always pleased to give his attention to his family. He would often take time away from administration to train us: Hana and me and my brothers. Mother would be his mock attacker as he demonstrated principles of fighting: the importance of distance between the fighters; how to watch your opponent; or when to move. These were my favorite times as a family. We would listen and learn, swords in our hands and our minds fixed on Father, privileged to know that we were being taught by the best warrior in the kingdom.

Now, as he heard our footsteps crunching across the gravel toward him, Father looked up and beamed with pleasure when he saw us all.

"Brother!" he cried, rising and coming to meet Uncle. "I welcome you."

They greeted each other formally at first, as befitted the *Jito* and a faithful servant. But soon Uncle was teasing my father just as he had teased Moriyasu, calling him by his childhood nickname of Koishi, which means "little stone."

My father laughed. "And as I recall," he reminded Uncle, "you were Oiwa, my 'big rock'! Always there to support me, Hidehira, just as now."

Patting his brother's shoulder, Father asked a servant to bring sake rice wine to refresh Uncle after his long journey. Then we all sat on tatami reed mats at my father's feet to listen as Uncle told us the news he'd gathered from patrolling my father's lands. I wished I was allowed to roam the countryside, fighting any bandits that I came across. What an exciting life!

The men talked for a long time and when I next looked up at the sky, I was surprised to see that the afternoon had turned to dusk. A handful of servants emerged from the pavilions and glided silently across the terrace gardens. They lit the lanterns that hung between the trees where they shone like small moons.

With a bow, Uncle withdrew to inspect his soldiers' weapons and my mother leaned forward to gently touch my hand. "Kimi," she murmured. "It's getting late. I would like you and Hana to take Moriyasu back to the bedchambers now."

"But I'd like to stay," I protested quietly. I glanced at my sister. "And I'm sure Hana would, too."

But my mother shook her head. "The men must prepare for their ceremonial dinner," she explained. "The *kaiseki ryori* is an important occasion during which your uncle will assume the duties of the *Jito* for your father."

"Uncle is to be *Jito*?" I asked my mother in surprise.

"Only temporarily," my mother said in a reassuring voice. "Just while your father travels around our estates with your older brothers. You remember our discussions about the journey Harumasa and Nobuaki must make, now that they are of an age to begin to understand the duties of their station? One day, one of your brothers will inherit the *Jito* title."

I did remember. We had talked many times, and not always peacefully.

But this time I didn't argue. Nor did I question why sons could inherit while daughters could not.

12

Instead I nodded, and did as my mother asked me.

But as soon as Moriyasu was settled with his nurse, I took Hana's hand and led her to the *shinden* banqueting room.

"What are you doing, Kimi?" she asked. "You know we mustn't disturb the ceremony."

"The ceremony will not be disturbed," I reassured her. "No one will even know we are there."

I led her quickly through the rooms to a hidden alcove I knew well, next to the formal dining room. The two of us hid easily behind the painted silk screen. I pressed my finger to my lips, signaling her to be quiet, and then pointed to a small slit at the edge of one of the padded sections.

Hana put her face to the slit, and then jumped back when she saw how close we were to the men. Her eyes were wide with amazement and delight, and I nodded—we would not be seen, but we could see everything!

There was a second slit for me to look through, and I could clearly see that my father, brothers, and uncle were kneeling on tatami mats just on the other side of the screen. Samurai soldiers sat shoulder to shoulder in two long lines that stretched all the way to the far walls of the banqueting room. All of them wore long, loose tunics. Those in red silk were Uncle's men, others in yellow served my father.

13

I felt a thrill of excitement as I watched the ceremony begin. They all washed their hands to purify themselves, and then my father began to speak. His words were thoughtful and formal, as befitted the ceremonial occasion.

"The house of Yamamoto is proud to welcome its treasured brother, Yamamoto no Hidehira," Father said, bowing to Uncle.

Uncle bowed low in response. I wondered how he felt, being welcomed to the place that had once been his own home . . . would still have been his home, if circumstances had been different. My grandfather had decided many years ago to pass the title of *Jito* to Father, even though he was the younger brother, because of his exceptional martial skill. Samurai from all over Japan came seeking work under my father's leadership. Since becoming the *Jito*, he has built strong alliances with neighbors that had once opposed our family, and has earned favor with the Shogun and the Emperor.

I was so proud of Father and all he had achieved. I prayed that I had inherited some of his skill, as my brothers had, and that one day we might all reach the standard he had set.

I gazed through the gap in the silk screen as Father turned to the gathered men. His voice rose with pride as he spoke of Hidehira's bravery in past battles. "My brother's skill was the key to defeating a rebel army from Shinano," he said. "He outfought three ambushes, and went on to march southward and defend our allies in the province of Sagami. The Yamamoto lands are in safe hands. Yamamoto no Hidehira will look after our people as if they were his own children."

Uncle bowed. "I thank you for the trust you place in me, brother. I am proud that you think me worthy of the great honor of passing your powers to me."

My father bowed. "You have earned that honor, Hidehira."

"Thank you, little brother," Uncle said.

Servants came gliding silently into the room, bearing balls of sticky rice, fresh sushi, and paper-thin slices of fresh soybean curd arranged on wooden trays shaped like leaves. They placed the food carefully on low black and gold lacquered tables, and then bowed as they withdrew backward from the room, their heads respectfully lowered.

I glanced at Hana and she made a face that said, "I'm hungry, too."

Using pairs of short *hashi* chopsticks, my father and Uncle helped themselves to bean curd and sticky rice. This was the part of the ceremony that took away the pangs of hunger that might spoil the enjoyment of tea drinking later.

15

When my father had finished, he passed his *hashi* to a waiting servant. "Hidehira, as you know, my sons will accompany me on my tour around the estates," he said to Uncle. "They are ready to learn about their inheritance, and to test the skills they have learned at their training school. Indeed we will be leaving early tomorrow morning to attend the opening ceremony at the dojo and pay our respects to Master Goku before we proceed on our tour."

"I trust that Goku has been as rigorous with them as he was with us, Koishi," Hidehira said.

"He has," my father replied. He glanced across at my eldest brother and raised his eyebrows. "As first son, perhaps you will demonstrate some of the moves Master Goku has taught you, Harumasa?"

My brother nodded eagerly and rose to his feet. I watched as he stepped into the wide space between the rows of tatami mats. "With your permission, I will now demonstrate."

Carefully drawing his long sword, Harumasa held the blade horizontally before his face and bowed to Father. Uncle sat back, a look of keen interest on his face.

Behind the silk screen, I mirrored Harumasa's graceful motions as he performed a series of slow movements to warm up. Knees bent . . . eyes on sword . . . elbow up . . . blade placed carefully

16

across the upturned palm of the hand, pointing to the floor. Every move was designed to concentrate the warrior's mind.

Now Harumasa was ready.

For a moment he looked as though he was preparing to dance, but then he executed a short, sharp, and deadly thrust.

Steel sword singing, Harumasa cut left and right, deflecting invisible attacks from an imaginary enemy. He bent at the knees and twisted behind to cover an attack from the rear. A turning single-handed forward slash was followed instantly by a fast two-handed slice. And when the invisible opponents were dead or dying from their wounds, Harumasa shook the imagined blood off his blade and sheathed his sword in one single fluid movement.

Behind the screen my hand followed his every move.

"Excellent," Uncle said as Harumasa bowed.

"Very good, first son," my father said, pride ringing in his voice as he gestured for my brother to sit down again. "You will earn the respect of the people we meet on our travels."

My heart burned at the unfairness. I had been dedicated in my training and practiced every day, even without the privilege of attending Master Goku's school. I had grown up watching Father's samurai exercises, copying the movements in the privacy of my bedchamber. Whenever my brothers were home from school, I had pestered them to teach me what they had learned. Now my skills were almost as polished as Harumasa's, but I would never have the chance to prove it.

One day, I promised myself, *I will show them that a girl can be just as good as a boy.*

For the hundredth time, I ached to be allowed to go on the journey around the province, riding with my father like my brothers. The arguments of the past moons played again in my head, and once more I heard my father's voice, kind but firm: "No, Kimi. As first daughter, it is your duty to remain here at your mother's side."

But I didn't want to be at my mother's side! I wanted to be out in the provinces on horseback, with the wind in my hair and a quiver of arrows strapped to my back. . . .

A sharp nudge from Hana brought me back to the present. Her expression showed that she knew I had been daydreaming. She mouthed, *Look,* and pointed to the slit in the screen. I looked through to see servants carrying in the charcoal fires to heat water for the tea. Others placed elegant ladles and small ceramic drinking bowls carefully on the low table in front of my father so that he and Uncle could admire them, as ceremony demanded.

My father made tea slowly and in silence, demonstrating with every move his authority and power as the *Jito*. I watched, fascinated as always by the strict rules of the tea ceremony.

His motions calm and harmonious, Father held his sleeve back with one hand as he poured a bowl of dark green tea and then lifted the bowl to his lips with both hands. He took a sip, wiped the rim, and then passed it to Uncle Hidehira who sipped in the same place to show their bond. The passing of the tea bowl symbolized the strong bond of friendship between them.

When he had finished, Uncle placed the bowl carefully on the mat in front of him. Then suddenly his red robes rippled as he rose to his feet and I felt a flash of surprise. Such abrupt movements were not fitting, especially during a tea ceremony!

"I honor my brother, the *Jito*," Uncle said. "Just as I honor our Yamamoto ancestors—especially our father, who chose to pass power to the little stone, Koishi, instead of the great rock, Oiwa."

Frowning, I looked at my father. His face showed the surprise and confusion that I too was feeling. What did Uncle mean—was he criticizing Grandfather's decision in front of everyone? I clenched my fists, my body full of tension.

However, Uncle smiled. I could see clearly as he pulled my father to his feet and embraced him. My father grunted and I guessed that he must have been astounded at such an unusual display of affection. But I relaxed, because all was well between them.

Then I realized that the grunt was not astonishment, but pain. My surprise turned quickly to shock as my father cried out. I caught a glimpse of his face. It was twisted in agony.

What was happening to him?

Then I looked at Uncle's hand and saw that he was holding the shiny red-lacquered hilt of his sharp *tanto* dagger. The blade was buried deep in my father's back . . . and a dark crimson stain was beginning to spread outward across the glossy yellow silk of his ceremonial robes.

CHAPTER TWO

As Uncle released him and stepped back, Father slumped heavily to the floor. His silk robes settled around him, hiding his face. My brothers Harumasa and Nobuaki leaped to their feet. Nobuaki paused to bend over my father, but there was nothing he could do. Our noble father was dead.

I shoved my fist against my mouth to stifle a scream as Harumasa turned on Uncle with a wild yell and drew his sword in a single sweeping movement.

Nobuaki leaped forward but was blocked by one of Uncle's samurai, a man with a battle-scarred face. Treacherous soldiers in red silk robes turned on those in yellow, and sharp cries tore the night air as clashes of swords echoed around the banqueting room. Uncle must have prepared them for this moment!

The look in Harumasa's eyes was terrifying as he prepared to attack. Hope swelled in me as he lunged at Uncle.

But Uncle was ready for him. Thrusting his own

ornate blade upward and outward, he easily parried Harumasa's swinging cut. Then he twisted away, slashing at my eldest brother with the *tanto* dagger he still held in the other hand—the dagger that still dripped my father's blood. Nobuaki, meanwhile, was still grappling with the battle-scarred samurai.

"Is that the best Master Goku could teach you?" Uncle sneered at Harumasa. "Killing you will be child's play!"

Killing you? Shock pounded through me and my skin turned cold as I caught a glimpse of Uncle's face. His expression was set and stern, his dark eyes those of a stranger. This was not my cheerful uncle, but a fearsome warrior determined to do battle— and win. He raised his sword and brought it down in a swooping curve.

Buckling under the assault, poor Harumasa tried to block the rain of attacks. His movements grew wilder, and he wasn't moving as quickly as he needed to. Nobuaki, still fighting hand to hand against the scarred samurai, yelled encouragement. I willed Harumasa to find the elegance and power that he had demonstrated earlier.

Harumasa managed to spin out from under Uncle's attack and raise his sword for a deadly slice, but Uncle was swift. With the tip of his blade pointing to the ground and the blade side facing my brother, Uncle put his left hand on the blunt side of his sword and pushed it upward and outward, before my brother could complete his advance. Then Harumasa was staggering backward, his face ashen with pain. Blood seeped across my brother's yellow tunic and I knew immediately that Uncle had sliced him from belly to throat.

I twisted my knuckles into my mouth, watching in horror as Uncle shoved Harumasa backward so that he crashed onto one of the black and gold lacquered tables.

Harumasa lay there for a moment, groaning.

And then my courageous brother was dead.

Seeing that Harumasa had been slain, my second brother, Nobuaki, roared with rage. He gave a swinging blow that knocked down the scarred samurai and allowed him to steal his attacker's still-sheathed sword. Then Nobuaki leaped at Uncle, wielding his enemy's weapon.

Nobuaki did not even land a blow, however, before my uncle coldly cut him down. With a sword in one hand and his lethal *tanto* blade in the other, Uncle outmaneuvered my second brother in a heartbeat.

Nobuaki's head shot back and bright blood spurted from his throat in a great red arc. His eyes widened and he pitched backward. He was dead before he hit the ground.

I wanted to leap into the fray and destroy my

uncle. But I had no weapon. Then Uncle kicked the sword from Nobuaki's lifeless hand. The blade came spinning across the room toward the silk screen—and in an instant I knew what I must do.

I must take up the sword and fight!

But before I could make a move, a distant scream echoed from beyond the *shinden*. The attack must have spread outside the banqueting room. Uncle wasn't just after my father and brothers!

I turned, heart racing, and found Hana was still at my side. She had been so silent that I'd almost forgotten she was there. Gentle Hana. Her face was as pale as a moonflower, her eyes enormous as she drank in the terrible scene. I grabbed at her, trying to pull her away. But she resisted, unable to tear her eyes from the bloodshed on the far side of the silk screen. I took her hand. It was soft and lifeless, as if all her bones had melted away and she was nothing more than a rag doll.

"Come on," I whispered, roughly squeezing her fingers. "We have to warn Mother and Moriyasu. *Now!*"

At the sound of my voice Hana blinked, like someone coming out of a trance.

"Now," she repeated, her eyes dark with pain. "Yes. We must go now."

We darted out from behind the screen, away from

the victorious cries of Uncle's samurai. Together we hurried along the corridor and just as we reached the corner, Uncle's gruff voice echoed from the banqueting room behind us.

"Find the rest of the family," he ordered his men. "Kill them all!"

There came the sound of paper walls tearing as samurai soldiers smashed their way out of the room. My heart beat hard with fear and for a terrible moment I thought my trembling legs would give way beneath me. *Come on,* I told myself. *Move!*

With Hana's hand gripped tight in my fist, I darted down one corridor and then the next, zigzagging through the *shinden* and out into the compound. I could hear Uncle's soldiers crashing into the courtyards and gardens. The harsh sound made me feel sick with terror.

Up ahead, a distant scream echoed again, and I knew it was coming from the bedchambers behind the *shinden.*

Is it Mother? I wondered. *Have soldiers reached her already? Please, no,* I prayed.

We ran faster, desperate to stay out of sight. All around us came the sound of massacre. Uncle's samurai showed no mercy, their battle cries mingling with the screams of pain coming from my father's samurai. I caught glimpses of shadows on the paper walls, like ghastly versions of the puppet shows Hana and I had watched as children. Swords sliced down on defenseless shoulders in the rooms as we passed. Blows rained on innocent heads. And blood flowed, splashing walls with gory crimson.

Hana and I came at last to a doorway that opened out onto a moonlit courtyard. It was deserted. Long shadows reached inky fingers across the paving stones. A solitary tree stretched slender branches to the night sky. I pressed myself against the door frame, and closed my eyes briefly.

"Why?" I whispered in distress. "Why would Uncle do this? We're his family! His own flesh and blood. I thought he *loved* us!"

Beside me, Hana choked back a sob. Her knees buckled and she almost fell. I grabbed her, slipping my arm around her waist and holding her tight.

"We must get to Mother and Moriyasu," I whispered. "Mother will know what to do." I glanced back over my shoulder, and then checked the courtyard again. "We can't let Uncle's samurai see us."

Hana was breathing heavily and I could feel her heart fluttering against the inside of my wrist like a tiny bird trying to escape its cage.

"Can you make it to the bedchambers?" I asked her.

Hana swallowed hard. "I'll try," she said, her voice hoarse.

"I'll count to three, and we'll go," I told her. "One . . . two . . . three . . ."

Crouching low, we darted to the nearest patch of shadow and paused, listening breathlessly for any sign that Uncle's soldiers had spotted us. I could hear shrill cries in another part of the compound, but nearby was nothing but silence.

We waited a moment, then I glanced at Hana, my eyebrows raised. She nodded and we set off again, leaving the fragile safety of the shadows and launching ourselves out into the moonlight.

Running, we made our way across the courtyard, then through a gateway carved like the spread wings of a crane, and onto a walkway that skirted the moss garden. Far away to our left, burning arrows flew toward our compound. Bright flames licked upward, illuminating the night sky.

"They're burning the pavilions," Hana gasped. "Why?"

"The fire will drive anyone who's hiding out into the open so they can be slaughtered," I said grimly.

We hurried on, and I tried to shut out the screams of the servants as they begged for their lives. Soon, fire raged through most of the compound, staining the sky red.

At last we came to our bedchambers.

We rushed up the steps and into the entrance

hall. Everything was quiet here, ominously still. A body was slumped in a doorway—a woman, dressed in a servant's simple blue cotton robe. I went down on one knee and turned her over. It was one of my mother's maids. Her throat had been cut.

I glanced up at Hana, terrified that we would enter Mother's rooms and find her dead, too. But I couldn't let terror stop me. I had to go on.

I stood up and took Hana's hand again. I forced myself to step over the maid's body and into my mother's bedchamber. The floor was wet beneath my feet and for a moment I thought someone had spilled a jug of water. But Hana's hoarse cry made me look down.

I realized we were standing in a pool of slick red blood.

Two more bodies lay slumped near the bed. I saw at a glance that neither of them was my mother. One was another young maid, her blue cotton robe soaked with blood, while the other was one of Uncle's samurai soldiers. His iron helmet had been wrenched off, and I guessed by the expression on his face that he'd died in pain. I felt no pity; he was a traitor to the *Jito* he had sworn to honor.

There had been a struggle. A small red and gold lacquered table had been smashed. Some of my mother's tiny pots of makeup were scattered across the mat. On the far side of the room, several of the cypress wood blinds that formed the wall had been torn down, and the cool breeze that drifted in from outside rippled the shreds of painted white silk inside.

And suddenly I saw something that made my heart leap.

Moriyasu's little wooden sword was on the floor by the gap in the wall!

CHAPTER THREE

I dashed across the bedchamber and picked up Moriyasu's sword.

My thoughts tumbled over one another. My little brother would never have left his beloved training weapon behind on purpose. He must have dropped it as he and Mother rushed away! Just holding it in my hand gave me a feeling of hope. Could they have escaped?

Cautiously I peered out of the gap in the blinds. The covered walkway that led along the side of the bedchambers and down to the ornamental lake was empty. To my relief, there were no bodies and no sign of blood.

"Mother and Moriyasu must have climbed out this way," I told Hana, tucking the little wooden sword into my sash. "Someone must have warned them. Come on, we must follow and see if we can find them."

Hana didn't reply.

I turned around and saw that she had sunk to the floor in the far corner of our mother's room. She was crouching, half curled into a ball, shivering as she buried her face in her hands.

I hurried over to her and pulled her into my arms. "Be strong, Hana," I whispered against her hair. "Just a little while longer. We'll find Mother and Moriyasu, and then everything will be all right. . . ."

"No, it won't," Hana said on a trembling breath. "Father is dead . . . Harumasa and Nobuaki are dead . . . things will never be all right again!"

"We must make them all right!" I said fiercely. "We have to get out of here, Hana. We have to survive and make sure that Uncle is punished for what he's done." I gave her a little shake. "We must be brave and put our emotions aside for now." I rested the back of my hand against her cheek. Her skin was cold. "Can you do that, Hana?" I asked. "Can you come with me to find Mother?"

She stared at me for a moment, her eyes so dark they were almost black. Then she nodded. "Swords," she said. "We'll need our swords if we have to fight."

"I'll go and get them," I said. "Stay here. Don't move until I come back."

The corridor was deserted and silent, but I could hear Uncle's soldiers nearby, tearing linen from the beds and slashing wall panels. They were searching for us. Careful not to make a sound, I tiptoed next door to the bedchamber I shared with Hana. Here, tables had been tipped over and our clothes ransacked. It made my heart ache to see Hana's scrolls of poetry torn to shreds and left on the floor.

I moved quickly, desperate to get back to Hana as soon as I could, in case the soldiers came back to check our rooms again.

Swiftly I took our swords from their ornate stand. Fashioned from tempered steel, the *nihonto* were long and lethally sharp but light and easy to carry in their wooden *saya* scabbards. I headed for the door—

And froze.

I heard the light scuff of boot leather on a floorboard. Someone was coming!

Shrinking back against the wall, I held my breath. I closed my eyes and concentrated my mind, trying to remember the rules of self-control from my training. My heart hammered so loudly that I was sure whoever was out there would hear it. *Breathe,* I told myself. *And don't panic.*

Though I had practiced often, self-control was hard to find when a real enemy was approaching. I had never fought an opponent with the intention of hurting them, but these soldiers did not have wooden *bokken*. Their sharp blades would be fatal.

My heart slowed. I listened again, ears straining to catch the slightest sound. This time I heard nothing except the distant cries of dying servants. Had I been mistaken?

No. There it was again. A quiet, creeping footstep. I opened my eyes and risked a peep through a crack in the door. One of Uncle's samurai was making his way slowly along the corridor. He stopped abruptly, just outside the doorway to my mother's chamber— where my sister sat alone and defenseless.

My fingers gripped the two *nihonto* in my left hand, and I swore to myself that I would kill the samurai if I had to.

He moved again, his leather armor creaking softly, and I wondered whether I could draw my sword without the sound alerting him to my presence.

Suddenly a shout echoed along the corridor. "Rokuro! This way!"

The samurai glanced back over his shoulder. I caught a glimpse of his face, under the shadow of his helmet. He was old, battle-hardened, with wrinkled skin and a red scar that puckered one corner of his mouth. He was the samurai who fought Nobuaki in the banqueting room.

"Not yet," he called back.

But a harsh voice insisted, "Now! Captain's orders."

The samurai glanced back at the doorway to

Mother's room. He hesitated, and for a moment I thought he was going to disobey orders.

My right hand tightened on the hilt of my sword. Silently I began to slide it from its scabbard.

But all at once the samurai changed his mind. He turned away. His armor and weapons clinked as he broke into a trot and hurried back the way he'd come.

Relieved, I waited until I was sure he was gone. Then I darted along the corridor, keeping close to the wall.

Hana was waiting where I had left her, crouched low with her arms wrapped around her slender body. She flinched when I entered the room, her face white with fear. But when she saw that it was me— and that I was carrying our *nihonto*—relief washed over her face.

"I heard a voice," she whispered.

"One of Uncle's samurai," I muttered, kneeling beside her. "He's gone now, but we may meet others—and if we do, we must be prepared to fight."

"I don't know if I have the strength." Hana's voice was so weak I could barely hear her.

"You must find it, somehow." I took her limp, cold hand and placed her sword firmly in her grip. I drew my own from its scabbard and weighed it in my hand, turning it this way and that so the steel caught the light. A sensation of power and confidence stole over me.

"Come on, Hana," I said quietly. "The safest way out is down by the lake. The path leads to the west gate, and eventually to the forest. We'll search for Mother and Moriyasu there."

I checked that none of Uncle's soldiers were on the walkway outside the gap, and then gathered my long skirts and hurried through the debris. Hana came after me, her sword gripped tightly in her hand. Keeping low, we made a dash for the lake.

The gardens were swathed in shadows, and I could hear the samurai on the other side of the buildings, shouting when they found a survivor. Flames licked upward and tall columns of orange sparks swirled into the sky. By morning, our home would be nothing but a charred and smoldering ruin.

There was no sign of Moriyasu or my mother near the lake. The water was black and still, not a ripple marred the onyx surface. I shivered and glanced at Hana.

"We'll do as you said, Kimi," she murmured. "The west gate . . . and then the forest."

Swords in our hands, we skirted around the edge of the lake and took a curving path to the west gate. The place was deserted. Father's guards must have rushed inside to join the fight against Uncle's samurai.

Hana and I hurried down the hill to the forest. But as we slipped among the trees, I heard a crashing sound in the darkness. Shouts echoed, and I knew that Uncle's men were nearby.

Stopping dead in my tracks, I tried to work out how many there were, and which way they were heading.

My heart sank as I realized a small army of Uncle's samurai were in the forest ahead.

And they were making straight for us!

Tightening my grip on my sword, I glanced back over my shoulder. The *shinden* and the buildings around it threw a curtain of crimson fire into the night sky. Even the rising moon looked blood red. We couldn't go back. But we couldn't go forward, either. I held my breath, trying to decide what to do.

An idea came into my mind like a whisper of soft summer wind.

The shrine . . .

I glanced at Hana and she nodded, as if she had read my mind. The shrine was a secret place in the heart of the forest, dedicated to our family god, where I sometimes went alone to practice with my sword. Thinking of it gave me strength and courage.

Uncle's samurai were coming closer, not caring

who heard them as they crashed through the undergrowth. Grabbing Hana's hand, I cut to the left and stayed low, half crouching and half running through the shadowy forest. Around us, the trees crowded closer. Bark gleamed silver in the moonlight. Dry leaves rustled and whispered. Soon the sounds of the soldiers fell far behind, and we were alone.

I knew we were near the shrine because we came to the *torii*, the gateway that marks the start of a sacred place. Two tall, slender pillars supported a carved crossbar, the ends curving upward like the wing tips of a bird in flight.

Hana and I stepped beneath the *torii*. We made our way on until we crossed the little wooden bridge over the stream and at last reached the tiny, open-fronted pavilion at the edge of a clearing.

"I think we'll be safe here," I murmured to Hana, sheathing my sword at last.

We bowed our heads and whispered a small prayer for the protection of our family, and then we stepped inside. There was a low wooden table with candles, a small iron lantern, and a scattering of yellow flowers and other offerings.

I noticed one offering had been misplaced. A small scroll had been rolled and hastily tied, without the careful knotting we usually used for luck, a hand's length away from the offering plate.

Hana dropped to her knees in front of the low table and gasped. She pointed to markings on the outside of the scroll that spelled out our names.

"It's for us," she said breathlessly. "And it's Mother's handwriting."

I glanced over her shoulder. Immediately I recognized the firm, confident sweeps of my mother's writing and I felt hope again.

Normally we would not touch an offering to the gods, but this seemed to have been put here for us. Hana carefully lifted the scroll and opened it slowly. "It's a poem."

"A poem?" My heart fluttered. "What does it say?"

"*Old branches break above and die . . . ,*" Hana read aloud, "*seedling grows thicker . . . the cherry blossom grows once more . . . new season begins.*"

"She would have known that we would come here if we managed to escape," I said. I read the poem again, trying to understand. "*Seedling grows thicker . . .* I wonder what she was trying to tell us."

"Moriyasu is the seedling," Hana said slowly. "Mother is telling us that although our father and older brothers are gone, our youngest brother is still alive. He will grow, and so our family tree will survive."

"Moriyasu is the future," I said, nodding. I touched my fingers briefly to the hilt of his little wooden

38

sword, still tucked in my sash. "He is hope. The 'new season' must mean winning back the seat of the *Jito* for Moriyasu, as Grandfather would have wished."

We couldn't know for sure that this was what Mother's message meant. But we had to hope for something, Hana and I. Without hope, there was nothing but loss and pain.

Hana glanced back over her shoulder, through the open front of the shrine to the dark forest beyond. "We must follow Mother and Moriyasu," she said. "But where do you think they've gone, Kimi?"

I thought for a moment. "Mother must know that Uncle will search for them as soon as he realizes they are not among the dead. Mother will need to go far away, to lose herself and Moriyasu . . . and what better place to become lost than in a crowded town?"

"Then the town is where we must go, too."

I nodded. "We'll rest here for the night, and set out at dawn."

Hana leaned forward. "We mustn't let the samurai see this," she said. "Or they will carry the news of our plans back to Uncle." She lit one of the offering candles and held the small scroll in the flame until it caught. She placed the burning paper on a stone plate and we watched as the orange flame turned our mother's parting message to black ash.

Once Mother's words were destroyed, I felt tiredness sweep through my body. I sank down and leaned against Hana, closing my eyes. At once images swarmed through my mind—the crimson stain spreading fast across my father's yellow silk robes . . . Harumasa's ashen face as he fell to the floor of the banqueting room . . .

And over those images echoed Uncle's last words to my father: "I honor my brother, the *Jito*," he had said. "Just as I honor our Yamamoto ancestors."

My heart ached as the memories washed over me, and silent tears ran down my face. How could Uncle have done this? Could he really be the same man who had taught me the *kata*? The laughing, affectionate uncle who had ridden on horseback with Hana and me, telling us stories of past battles? Desolation gripped me as I remembered one long-ago summer's day when our whole family had taken a picnic down to the river. Moriyasu had been a baby then, swaddled in a silk robe in Mother's arms. Hana and I had been little girls playing in the water, splashing our cousin Ken-ichi, while Uncle and Father had laughed and joked together on the river-bank. I could hardly believe how our family had been torn apart.

I felt Hana slip her arms around me, and soon her tears were wet on my shoulder. We wept for a long time, kneeling at the shrine of our ancestors. Outside, the moon climbed high in the sky. The black of night grew deeper in the forest.

Eventually Hana and I curled up together on the mat. Lulled by the soothing sound of the nearby stream, we slept.

I sat bolt upright, heart pounding. I didn't know how long I'd been asleep, but something had woken me.

There! There was the sound again—a dry twig snapping under the weight of a heavy boot.

Beside me, Hana was leaning on one elbow, her eyes wide. Another branch cracked, and then came the unmistakable sound of creeping footsteps.

Hana glanced up at me and mouthed silently, *Someone's coming!*

I reached out a hand and quietly gripped the hilt of my *nihonto*. I was ready to defend us both, to the death if need be.

The footsteps crept closer. Silently I slid my sword from its scabbard.

I crept toward the entrance, held my breath, and waited . . .

Suddenly the intruder loomed in the open doorway. Moonlight glinted on his elaborate iron samurai helmet and I knew that this was one of Uncle's men. Before I could make a move, he shot out an

41

arm and grabbed my throat. His fingers were like a steel vice around my neck as he dragged me out of the shrine. I began to choke.

I staggered but he kept me upright, his face so close to mine that I could smell the fish on his breath. I stared into his battle-hardened face and the long red scar that puckered one corner of his mouth, and realized that this was the samurai who had crept along the corridor to my mother's chamber earlier. My hand gripped tighter on the hilt of my sword.

"I've been tracking you silly girls since you left the banqueting hall." He sneered. "And you never suspected a thing." He sniggered, a nasty, low, rasping sound, and tightened his grip on my throat.

I couldn't breathe. Blood pounded in my ears.

As he raised the point of his sword to my throat he whispered, "I will be well rewarded for killing you!"

CHAPTER FOUR

"Not as easy as you think," I gasped.

I flung my sword up toward his head. The sharp edge near the hand guard sliced easily through the leather flap at the side of his helmet. Crimson blood spurted from the side of his face and for a moment he was blinded, shrieking in agony. His grip on my throat loosened and I twisted away.

He staggered toward me, blinking the blood from his eyes. I half turned, moving fast, and jerked my elbow up under his chin. His head snapped back and my sudden small victory gave me courage. Power surged through my limbs as I leaped forward into the air, my foot swinging up to deliver a hard kick—

But the samurai stepped behind me and grabbed my shoulder. He pulled hard and all at once I was falling! I landed flat on my back in the dirt, the breath knocked from my body.

With a sneer of triumph, he brought his boot down

hard on my sword arm. Pain lanced through me.

"You will die on my blade," the samurai muttered, black eyes glittering from the shadows beneath his helmet.

I struggled and tried to break free, but I was trapped. Somewhere nearby, I heard the metallic whisper of another sword being drawn. *Had more samurai come for us?*

Suddenly I caught a glimpse of a pale figure running from the shadows of the shrine, hands clasped together around the hilt of a silvery blade, silky black hair trailing behind. *Hana!* She sprinted across the clearing and swung at the old soldier.

The samurai cursed and twisted like a cat to face her, stepping off my arm. He deflected her attack with his blade, and the clash of steel echoed through the forest.

I scrambled to my feet. The samurai's back was to me, so I rushed at him with a downward slice of my sword. He must have heard me coming because he stepped away, and I could only catch him with a sharp slash to the forearm.

The samurai howled and turned with a fast, high, sideways slice but I ducked before it could take my head off my shoulders. I had hit him twice now.

Moonlight flashed on flat steel. Hana came at him from the other side but he deflected her blow. As he moved, I saw the leather laces that held the steel plates of his armor together pull apart to reveal his patterned kimono. Beneath would be his flesh. The perfect place to strike . . .

As if he sensed my intent, the samurai turned and came at me in a roaring attack, sword whirling above his head. He had murder in his eyes, and in that instant I knew that his would be a fatal blow. "Victory!" he yelled.

Without hesitation, I stepped to the side and flung my weapon up to knock his away. The force sent shudders jarring down my arm.

The samurai's own weight and the ferocity of his charge brought him forward, bellowing. Quickly I dropped down on one knee and plunged my sword into his side. My sharpened steel slipped cleanly into the gap between the plates of armor—and my blade was buried in his flesh.

He turned toward me in surprise and for a moment we stared at each other, eye to eye, his hot breath whistling into my face. "I may bleed," he hissed, "but I won't die. Not until I've killed you!" Then he rammed his body farther onto my blade.

The samurai gasped for breath, sending a fine spray of blood across my face. I let out a horrified cry.

He raised his sword and would have brought it swinging down, its silver arc aimed for my head. But abruptly Hana was there, her *nihonto* swirling through the air. Her blade sliced through the samurai's wrist.

He howled in agony as his severed hand fell to the ground. His eyes bulged. I could feel his weight dragging on my sword, twisting the blade inside him even more. "You won't last long . . . ," he rasped. "He will find you."

Gulping back my horror, I staggered backward and my blade came free.

The samurai fell to his knees, both hands clutching at his side. A single labored breath wheezed from between his lips, then his eyes glazed. He toppled sideways onto the ground and then was still.

For a moment the world seemed to swing around me. Reeling, I looked for Hana. She was standing a few paces away, her eyes wide with shock. Our eyes met and locked. Hers were black whirlpools of confusion and despair. She tore her gaze away and looked down at her bloodied sword hanging limply in her hand. Without warning her knees buckled. . . .

I dropped my own sword and leaped toward her, catching her just before she hit the ground. Gently I lowered her down.

"We k-killed him, Kimi," she stammered.

"We had to," I told her fiercely. "Otherwise *he* would have killed *us*!"

The moon disappeared behind a bank of ragged

cloud and the clearing was plunged into shadow. Hana's hand groped for mine and we clung to each other in the darkness.

"Our lives will never be the same," she whispered at last.

I swallowed hard. "We have a future, though," I said firmly. "Once we find Mother and Moriyasu."

All around us, a breeze stirred through the trees. Hana sprang away from me, staring wildly into the blackness.

"Someone's there!" Hana whispered. "Uncle has sent more men to look for us. They'll find us, and kill us—"

"No one's there," I interrupted. I glanced over my shoulder, scanning the trees until I was sure. "It's just the wind."

Beside me, Hana shuddered. I turned back to her. "Hana, be strong. We mustn't let ourselves be overcome by sadness or pain."

She buried her face in her hands and began to cry. She looked so broken. How could I help her?

"Do you remember that little lacquered box we used to keep on a shelf in our room?" I asked, gently stroking her hair. "It had a golden willow tree on the lid. . . ."

For a moment I thought she hadn't heard me, but then she took her hands away from her face and looked up at me. Tears glistened on her cheeks, but she wasn't crying anymore.

"Imagine that you hold that box in your hands now," I told her. "Imagine yourself opening it up and packing all your fear and sadness inside. Close the lid, Hana, and put the box away on a high shelf . . . in a dark place where you can't see it." I took her hands and held them tight. "Leave the box there with your fear packed away. Now we know nothing of fear. Only survival. We must get away from here, go to the town, and somehow find Mother and Moriyasu."

Hana closed her eyes for a moment. When she opened them again, her face was strong. "We'll survive," she said. "And strike down those who bring dishonor to the name of Yamamoto."

I nodded. For a moment I gazed around at the land that used to belong to our father. To our family. *Yamamoto* . . . the name seemed to echo in my mind, whispered through the trees around the clearing. All at once, I realized that Uncle had even stolen our name. Hana and I could no longer be Yamamoto.

"We must forget who we are," I said. "Leave the name of Yamamoto behind when we leave this place."

"Why?" Hana stared at me, her eyes wide. "What do you mean?"

"Because our name will make it too easy for Uncle's soldiers to find us," I explained. "We can no longer be the daughters of the *Jito*."

48

"But how can we stop being daughters of the *Jito*?" Hana asked, smoothing the front of her sea-green kimono with trembling hands. "People will know who we are just by looking at us."

I stared at her for a moment as the thoughts chased one another through my mind. Then a sudden flash of inspiration hit me. "We'll disguise ourselves," I said eagerly. "Change our clothes . . . make our faces dirty . . ." I clenched my fist and glanced across at the dead samurai. "Uncle's men will be looking for two *girls*. So we'll become *boys*. We'll twist up our hair into topknots, just like our—" I broke off and swallowed hard. I had been about to say, *Just like our brothers do.* As if they were still alive. "Just like our brothers *did*," I finished helplessly.

Hana reached out and clasped my hand. "That's a good idea," she said. "If anyone asks, we can say we're the sons of a poor farmer on our way to the town to look for work."

I glanced across at the dead samurai and swallowed hard. "Could you bear to put on some of his clothes?"

She was silent for a moment, her eyes fixed on my face. Eventually she nodded. "I'll do what I have to," she said firmly.

I got to my feet and went over to the dead samurai. His helmet was tipped back away from his face, his mouth stretched wide as if he'd died crying out.

I dropped to my knees and reached out with my hands, half expecting him to snarl at me, or sit up and thrust a blade into my heart. I knew I had killed this man, but somehow it didn't seem real.

Hana came to kneel beside me. "Here, let me help you," she said, and placed her hands over mine. Together we began to unlace his hardened leather armor.

"Can we use this?" Hana asked, weighing the heavy breastplate in her hands. "It might protect us."

I shook my head. "Farmers' sons don't wear armor," I said regretfully. "But we can use most of his clothes."

Quickly we tossed aside the breastplate and the samurai's heavy sleeve armor. Underneath, his kimono jacket was patterned blue and black, with short sleeves and a narrow sash. His *hakama* trousers were gray, tied in at the knee, and full of lice.

Hana made a face and held them at arm's length. "These are disgusting!"

"And I always thought the life of a samurai soldier was glamorous!" I muttered, managing a grin.

I sat back on my heels and spread the kimono jacket out across the ground. It was covered in blood and had a slit where my sword had gone through. "We'll take everything down to the stream and wash it," I said. "It's a warm night and the

50

clothes will dry as we wear them."

We scooped up the clothes, gathered our swords, and made our way through the trees to the stream. There was soft moss beneath my knees as I kneeled down and washed the blood from the kimono. Hana scrubbed at the *hakama* trousers with a handful of grit from the streambed. It was a relief to lose ourselves in the simple task.

Quickly I stripped down to my own blue cotton *hakama* trousers and put on the kimono. The wet fabric clung to my skin like icy fingers as I folded it carefully to hide the slit. I firmly knotted the sash around my waist, then sheathed my *nihonto* and fastened it into the sash next to Moriyasu's little wooden sword. Finally I tied my long hair up into a tall topknot the way I had seen my brothers arrange theirs.

When I had finished, I helped Hana take off her sea-green silk and replace it with the dead samurai's plain gray *hakama*. The cold fabric made her shiver. "I'm glad it's a warm night," she said as she finished tying her hair into a topknot.

I nodded. "We're lucky it's almost spring and not the middle of winter."

Underneath her kimono Hana was wearing a white undershirt, but it looked too clean against the dull gray of the samurai's *hakama* so I scooped up

51

moss and mud to smear across the sleeves and collar.

"There . . . ," I said at last, standing back to gaze at her in the half light of the moon. "You do look like a boy."

"So do you." Hana reached up and briefly touched her hair. "What should we do with our own clothes?" she asked. "Should we bury them?"

"No, we haven't got time. Let's sink them in the stream."

Together we wrapped our old clothes around heavy rocks and shoved them under the water, tucking them beneath an overhanging lip of earth where they wouldn't be found. I couldn't help but think that in abandoning my robes, I was also abandoning the last remnants of my identity as a Yamamoto lady.

When the clothes had sunk from sight, I made a silent promise that one day I would reclaim my family name and honor.

Whatever it took.

Then I reached for my sister's hand—our journey had begun.

CHAPTER FIVE

Afraid that we might meet more of Uncle's samurai, we stayed away from the pathways that cut through the forest. As we walked, the tangled undergrowth and branches tore at our hair and clothes. We kept the moon on our right hand side, and used a single star to guide us west, toward the town.

Soon our ravaged home was far behind us.

The only sound was the occasional scrabble of an animal or the hoot of an owl. As we walked, I thought about Mother and Moriyasu. Were they far ahead of us? Had they found a horse or had someone helped them? Were they injured or did Mother have everything under control?

Sometime during the night the moon disappeared and darkness closed in around us. My straw sandals broke and I had to go barefoot. My belly was tight with hunger, my mouth parched. Hana trudged bravely beside me, her head down, wrapped in her own thoughts.

At last we found ourselves standing hand in hand at the edge of the trees on the crest of a steep hill. Dawn was just breaking across the eastern sky, pink and bright.

Below us stretched rice fields where farmers in flat straw hats were already paddling through the shallow silver water to tend their crops. A narrow dirt road lined with small bamboo groves snaked away to the right and disappeared behind a series of low hills. Tiny huts were clustered at the side of the road with smoke rising from square holes cut into the thatched roofs.

Hana sniffed the air. "I can smell rice boiling," she said. "And fish soup. Do you think the villagers would share their food with us?"

"They might if we offer to do a few jobs," I said. "We could work in return for a meal."

Our hearts full of hope, we stepped out from the shelter of the trees and began to make our way down the hill toward the village.

We had almost reached the road when the air was filled with the thunderous sound of horses' hooves—and all at once a mass of samurai horsemen came galloping around a bend in the road. The rising sun behind them glittered from the tips of their spears and from the quivers of arrows strapped to their backs.

54

Hana grabbed my sleeve. "Uncle's men!" she whispered frantically, and we made a dash for the nearest grove of bamboo.

We crouched in the dust as the horsemen galloped closer and closer. Had they seen us? And if they did, would our disguises fool them into believing that we were just two simple boys?

I held my breath. Hana's fingers dug hard into my arm. The horsemen drew level, their horses' hooves drumming the earth. But they passed us by, only reining in when they reached the village.

Hana and I watched through the fronds of bamboo as a few women and children came hurrying out of their houses. They fell to their knees in the dirt, bowing low.

Several of the samurai leaped off their horses. Harsh voices echoed on the breeze, carrying across the dusty road to where we were hiding. Hana and I were just close enough to hear what they were saying.

"Has anyone passed through here this morning?" asked one of the samurai. I could see he was a captain by the red silk sash tied around his upper arm. "We're looking for slaves, runaways from the *Jito*'s household who are accused of stealing. They must be captured and punished."

Hana and I looked at each other indignantly.

Uncle was telling everyone that we were thieves!

Across the road, an old woman lifted her head from the dirt. "We've seen no travelers since yesterday morning," she said.

The captain of the samurai stepped closer to her and put the toe of his boot beneath her chin, lifting her face so that he could stare down at her. "Think carefully, old woman," he snarled, "because if you're lying it will mean death for you—and for your family." His hand went to the hilt of his sword.

"I swear!" the old woman wailed. "I've seen no one."

The captain glared down at her for a moment longer, then abruptly let her go and signaled to his soldiers. They swarmed through the village and searched the houses. Bedding was tossed out into the mud. Pots and pans clattered. Children ran to their mothers.

I seethed with rage. These people didn't deserve this! I wanted to leap up, dash out of the shelter of the bamboo, and attack the nearest samurai with my sword. But against all of them it would mean certain death. And besides, Hana had her hand on my arm to restrain me. She knew me so well.

The farmers began to hurry back across the paddy fields, wading through the water. One man who seemed like the head villager began to shout angrily, waving his arms as he approached.

The captain of the samurai waited until the head villager drew near. I saw his hand drift to the hilt of his sword.

A samurai never draws his sword unless he intends to use it, I thought, my heart beginning to race.

Calmly the captain grabbed his sword and swept his blade sideways in a glittering arc to slice the man's head from his shoulders. It hit the ground with a dull *thunk*.

Beside me, Hana sucked in her breath. "Why?" she whispered, as the sound of wailing carried across the road to us.

"I think it's a lesson," I said grimly. "They want the villagers to know what happens to anyone who might help us. We can't go down there, Hana. Not even after the samurai have gone. No one will help us now. . . ."

We waited until the samurai had galloped away. The villagers carried the dead man inside the nearest house and soon the place was deserted.

"Let's go back to the trees," I whispered to Hana.

Quickly we slipped out from the cover of the bamboo grove, feeling vulnerable as we scrambled back up the slope. Soon we were back in the safety of the forest. No one could see us now, even if they were looking.

In silence we skirted the hillside, keeping the

village on our right. I wanted to get as far away from those soldiers as I could. As we walked, I wondered how we would survive without shelter or food. How far away was the town—a day's walk?

"We'll sleep during the day," I told Hana as we trudged through the undergrowth. "Walk by night and pray that we come across another stream or river where we can get water. Maybe we'll find some mushrooms and berries in the forest to eat. We have to be invisible."

Hana nodded. Her eyes were dark with exhaustion and I knew we had to sleep soon. But where?

On the other side of the hill, the forest curved downward away from us and then swept up in an endless carpet of lush green. Just visible among the trees on the brow of the next hill was a complex of curving red rooftops.

Was that a pavilion? Or—

"A dojo!" Hana cried breathlessly. "A samurai training school!"

There was only one dojo in this part of the province—Master Goku's. The school my brothers had attended. "We could go to the gates and beg for food," I said.

"But what if Uncle's samurai have gotten there before us?" Hana asked.

I bit my lip, thinking for a moment. "They were

heading north, toward the town," I reasoned. "This is in the opposite direction."

"That's a big risk to take," Hana said, frowning. "What if Uncle sent out more than one search party?"

I gazed across the green valley to the curving red rooftops. Something seemed to draw me there, as if a silent voice was telling me that this was our chance to disappear. Our brothers had been students at this school, and Father before them. If they had still been alive, then this is where they would have been heading today, because this had been the first stop on their tour of the province.

Perhaps it was karma for Hana and me to come across the dojo.

Harumasa and Nobuaki had described their daily life to me so often that I knew their schedules by heart. They had endured hours of rigorous training alongside a hundred other boys, as well as a strict timetable of Zen studies. I had been thrilled by their tales of hand-to-hand combat and their eager discussions about battle tactics, weapons training, and martial skills. From dawn until dusk they did little else but fight, which meant that a dojo was the last place that Uncle's men would come looking for two noble young ladies.

Slowly a plan began to form in my mind.

"If we presented ourselves at the gate as two poor

farm boys seeking to train under a great master, then maybe we could do more than find food there." I spoke quickly to keep pace with my train of thought. "Perhaps we could stay longer . . . have a roof over our heads until Uncle's soldiers gave up their search. We would be *safe*."

Hana nodded, her face brightening. "Staying at the dojo would give us time," she acknowledged. "We can think of what to do next, and how we're going to find Mother and Moriyasu."

"And if we prove ourselves worthy of training," I went on, "there might be a chance for us to improve our sword skills. Then, if we are given an opportunity to challenge Uncle, we'll be able to show him exactly what happens to those who disgrace the name of Yamamoto."

"Do you think it will work?" Hana asked. She put up a hand and touched her topknot. "Do we *really* look like boys, Kimi?"

"Of course we do," I said firmly. "We'll be very careful, talk in deeper voices, and make sure we don't make the slightest mistake to give anything away."

"Okay." Hana reached out to grasp my hand. "Let's try," she said, and began to lead the way.

Fresh breezes stirred the trees as we hurried down one hill and up the next, following a dusty road that wound through the forest like a brown ribbon. A flock of cranes flew overhead, reminding me of one of the paintings on the silk screens at home, but I pushed the memories away . . . and at last we came to the dojo.

A high stone wall ran alongside the road and in the middle, an enormous solid wood gate stood at least three times the height of a man. Two guards in leather armor stood at attention, one on each side, glittering spears in their hands. They glared at us from beneath the peaks of their iron helmets as we stepped out from the shadow of the trees.

I took a deep breath and put my hand on the hilt of Moriyasu's little wooden sword to give me courage. Then I stepped toward the nearest guard.

His hand tightened on his spear and for a moment I thought he was going to lower it and run me through—

But just then, a small door set into the gates flew open.

I gulped back my relief as three boys of my own age came tumbling out through the doorway, laughing and jostling one another, the hems of their long black *hakama* trousers swirling in the dust.

One of them had a long, ornate sword fastened tightly at his waist by a blue silk sash. He had clever dark eyes, wide cheekbones, and a firm mouth. And even though I had not seen him for almost five years, he looked enough like his father for me to know that this was my cousin Ken-ichi—the only son of my treacherous uncle Hidehira.

My skin turned cold with fear.

CHAPTER SIX

Ken-ichi caught sight of me and I quickly tucked my chin down, praying that he wouldn't recognize us. For a moment there was silence; then he swaggered toward me and stared down at my bare feet.

"A peasant boy, eh?" he said slowly. "Surely you aren't stupid enough to think you might be able to join our training school?"

His voice was heavy with arrogance, and I glanced up at him from beneath my lashes. Ken-ichi had changed. What had happened to the boy I used to know? The good-natured cousin who used to laugh with me when we were children?

"Looks like he *is* stupid, Ken-ichi," one of his friends said with a snigger. "Why else would he be here?"

Ken-ichi walked a full circle around me, studying me from head to toe. An insect buzzed near my face and I wanted to swat it away but I didn't dare move.

Ken-ichi paused to look at Moriyasu's little wooden sword and gave a snort of laughter. "Is that what they teach you to fight with out in the paddy fields?" he asked. "How old are you? Five years? Six?"

"I'm thirteen," I said fiercely, remembering just in time to make my voice sound deeper and more like a boy's. "And I have a sword."

Ken-ichi nodded. "I can see that," he said, bending down to inspect my *nihonto*. "Tempered steel blade . . . carved hilt . . . a scabbard worthy of the finest craftsmen . . . but I don't think that sword is really yours, is it? A blade like that is far too good for a stinking peasant like you. You stole it!"

"I did not!" I protested. How could I have been so stupid? He was right! A peasant wouldn't have a *nihonto* like mine. "It was a gift from my father," I said quickly.

Ken-ichi shrugged. "Then your father's a thief," he said in a matter-of-fact way, and circled around me again.

I wanted to launch myself at him and make him apologize . . . but I controlled myself. Attacking a student of the dojo wasn't the way to get an interview with the Master. I gritted my teeth and turned to address the guard.

But Ken-ichi put himself in front of me again. "The most noble families in the kingdom of Japan

64

send their sons to train here," he drawled. "And nobles like *us* don't mix with stinking peasants like *you*."

I should have been angry when he said that, but I knew him calling me a stinking peasant was proof that he hadn't recognized me. I relaxed, just a little, and forced myself to unclench my fists.

"You two had better get lost," Ken-ichi said, glancing across at Hana. When he looked at her, Hana dipped her head and stared down at the road. "Go on—get lost," he said, his voice louder now. "Back to the paddy fields with you."

Ken-ichi had changed so much. The last time I had seen him he had been a boy, listening thoughtfully as my father read poetry to us both in a sun-drenched courtyard. Now many moons had passed, and Ken-ichi had turned into an arrogant young man who sneered at strangers. I wondered briefly what had happened to make him like this. Then another thought occurred to me. Did Ken-ichi even know that my father was dead? Was he aware of what his own father had done?

I decided to test him—to mention Father and watch Ken-ichi to see what his reaction was.

"I beg your forgiveness, sir," I said in a respectful tone, bowing low. "We are two humble boys, strangers to the province. We seek only to improve our skills and heard that the *Jito*, Lord Steward Yoshijiro, sent his sons to this dojo."

Ken-ichi didn't flinch when I said Father's name. "That's true," he said with a shrug. "Harumasa and Nobuaki are students here. What of it?"

His tone was easy and natural, and I was certain that he had no idea that my father and brothers were dead. I bowed lower. "If the sons of the *Jito* were students here, then this must indeed be a very great dojo."

"It's the best in all Japan," Ken-ichi said proudly. "Too good for the likes of you. Now get out of the way, rice boy. My friends and I have an appointment in the village, and you've delayed us long enough."

With that, Ken-ichi beckoned to his friends and deliberately shoved past me, coming so close that the *saya* scabbards of our swords clashed together. The harsh sound echoed in the clear morning air.

I froze. Ken-ichi and his friends whirled around and the nearby guards stared at us, their eyes wide with shock. A clash of *saya* was a grave insult to any samurai, student or not.

I glanced at Ken-ichi. His eyes were as sharp as swords. "How dare you!" he hissed, his face growing red with fury. "You—you—*stinking peasant!*"

I was sick of being called a peasant, and I felt my temper rise. "It was your fault!" I exclaimed, fists clenched in the folds of my *hakama* trousers. "You pushed past me!"

"I am the nephew of the *Jito*," Ken-ichi retorted. "You should have shown me respect by backing off and going down on your knees while I passed by."

"I don't go down on my knees to anyone," I muttered fiercely.

"Then perhaps it's time you did," Ken-ichi said. He drew his sword in a single fluid movement. "You've come here to learn, have you? Then I'll give you a lesson in *respect*, rice boy. Draw your blade!"

The guards stared blankly ahead as if they had suddenly gone blind. A breeze shifted through the pine trees behind me.

Ken-ichi glared at me. "We fight to first blood."

I exchanged a glance with Hana. Her mouth was set in a grim line and her hand was on the hilt of her *nihonto*. As if they sensed she would come to my aid, Ken-ichi's two friends moved quickly, blocking her. She tried to step around them, but one of them shot out an arm and held her back.

I turned back to Ken-ichi and quickly drew my sword.

Ken-ichi stared back at me. "First blood, rice boy," he said again.

I tested the weight of my *nihonto*. The hilt felt smooth and familiar in my hand, the steel perfectly balanced. I slid my right foot backward and stared at Ken-ichi, trying to read him as he shifted his weight and took a two-handed grip on his sword.

He let out a bloodcurdling yell and came at me hard and fast. The tip of his blade glittered in the sunshine as it sliced the air. I brought my *nihonto* up in a high deflection. Steel clashed on steel, the sound echoing from the walls surrounding the dojo.

Ken-ichi showed me no mercy, and I expected none. He was a good fighter—better than I expected—every bit as swift and skillful as my brothers had been. His dark eyes fixed on me; he came at me with quick, fluid attacks, fueled by anger and aggression that he only just kept under control. I was forced to block again and then quickly slide my right foot forward, keeping my stance strong as I raised my blade and brought it slicing down.

Our swords crossed and then twisted together, blades ringing, the sound carrying in through the open gate of the dojo.

Ken-ichi didn't let a single opportunity slide by— he attacked the merest hint of an opening, and only frantic rolling of my wrists enabled me to swing my blade back to deflect his attempted strikes.

I caught a brief glimpse of Hana watching us with a terrified gaze. Ken-ichi's friends called encouragement to Ken-ichi as they held Hana back. One of them had seized her sword and twisted it from her grasp. Her face was flushed as she struggled against them.

Breathless now, Ken-ichi and I danced around each other, the dust on the road churning beneath our feet. He was quick and light, his blade flashing up and then downward in a glittering arc. My cousin's years of training here at the dojo showed in his smooth, purposeful movements. I felt a sudden stab of fear. How could I hope to defeat him?

Desperately fighting back, I kept my gaze fixed on Ken-ichi's swinging blade. I could hear myself grunting as our swords jarred together. The midday sun beat down on our heads and I felt sweat prickle across my forehead.

Again and again, our blades sang through the air, upward, sideways, back, down. I shot one hand straight out in front of me, struggling to keep myself centered while my sword hand flashed upward— and suddenly Ken-ichi ducked beneath my blade and came in so close I felt his arm touch mine. He grasped the handle of my *nihonto* and twisted hard.

The next moment I was flying through the air and landed hard on the dusty road, the breath knocked from my body. Knowing that I must get up again, I tried to stand. But it was too late. A shadow fell across me. Ken-ichi was there, blocking out the sunlight as he loomed over me. His sneer was triumphant as he slowly brought his sword down and placed the blade against my cheek.

"Remember the rules, rice boy," he said softly. "First blood . . ."

"No!" Hana cried in horror, struggling harder against Ken-ichi's friends.

But Ken-ichi ignored her. I could feel the razor-sharp edge of his sword pressing into the soft skin just beneath my eye. I gritted my teeth and told myself that I would not beg my cousin for mercy.

All at once a loud and commanding voice cut the air around us. *"Stop!"*

Immediately Ken-ichi sprang back. I glanced up and saw a man standing calmly in the gateway of the dojo. Gray-haired with bushy gray eyebrows, he was dressed in a long black silk kimono belted with a wide black sash. With his straight back and strong shoulders, he did not seem like an old man. His face was stern.

At the sight of him, Ken-ichi hastily sheathed his sword. Ken-ichi's friends let Hana go. One of them tossed her sword down into the dirt as I scrambled to my feet.

Ken-ichi bowed low. Although I had never seen the man before I guessed that this must be Master Goku. He had taught my father and my brothers, and Father had often spoken of his wisdom and skill.

"I heard the clash of swords as I led my class in meditation," Master Goku said in a quiet, measured tone. "I thought that perhaps bandits had dared to come to the gates of my training school. Naturally I hurried to investigate." He stared at Ken-ichi with narrow dark eyes. "But on my arrival I see no bandits. Merely boys. Perhaps, Ken-ichi, you could explain to me what is going on here?"

"This peasant insulted me, Master Goku," Ken-ichi replied. His ferocity was gone now that he thought he might be in trouble with the Master, and I saw a glimpse of the cousin I used to know. "He did not move aside to let me pass on the road."

"Is that so?" Master Goku's stern gaze rested on me for a moment. "Did you insult my student, boy?"

"I meant no insult," I said quietly. "Our swords touched, but it was an accident."

Ken-ichi snorted and would have protested, but Master Goku silenced him by raising one hand. "It is easy to see the worst in any action," he said thoughtfully. "A good samurai should know the difference between an insult and an accident, and avoid violence until it is necessary." He folded his hands inside his wide sleeves and settled his gaze on Ken-ichi. His eyes were as dark as black slate. "If you are ever to be a samurai, then you must learn to control your pride."

Ken-ichi's bow deepened. "Yes, Goku-sensei," he

murmured, using a respectful term of address.

"Go now, and meditate upon the folly of rash actions." Master Goku waved his hand toward the doorway that led into the dojo.

"But this is my free hour, Master Goku," Ken-ichi spluttered. "We're going to the village—"

Master Goku silenced him with a stern look. "I have asked you to meditate, Ken-ichi. You and your friends go back into the school. Immediately."

Ken-ichi shot me a furious glare and then stomped back through the gate and into the dojo with his friends.

I looked back at Master Goku and found his gaze was fixed on me. "Sheath your sword, boy." His command was quiet, but left no doubt that it was to be obeyed.

I hadn't realized until then that my *nihonto* was still in my hand, and I quickly returned it to its scabbard.

"Now, tell me what you are doing here at my gates," Master Goku said.

I wasn't sure, but his voice seemed gentler than when he had spoken to Ken-ichi. I swallowed hard and bowed. Beside me, Hana bowed, too.

"Please forgive the intrusion, Master," I said. "We are two humble boys who have come from far across the province to seek a place in your training school."

Master Goku smiled. "I am honored that you have

72

traveled so far to attend my school," he said. "But I'm afraid you have wasted your journey. My dojo is full, and there are many boys waiting for places to become free." He bowed. "You must seek a place in one of the other schools. I wish you good luck."

With that, he turned to go back inside.

Hana threw a desperate glance at me and stepped forward. The guards quickly crossed their spears, blocking her so that she could not go after Master Goku.

"Wait, Master," she called. "Hear our plea."

Master Goku stopped in his tracks. He did not turn around, but he seemed to be listening.

Hana took a deep breath. "My brother and I do not wish to train in any other school," she said firmly. "For us, there is no other dojo but this one."

The guards glared as I went to stand beside her. "We have great potential as warriors," I put in. "Would you give us a chance to show you that we're worthy of a place in the best school in the kingdom?"

Master Goku slowly turned around to look at us.

"Please let us show you our skills, Master Goku-san," I went on. "My brother and I have practiced hard . . . and we could match any of your students in one-to-one combat if that's what it would take to prove our worth."

"Belief in the self is an admirable quality in a

warrior," Master Goku said. "One should never approach combat with any element of doubt in one's own skills."

He looked at us both in silence for a long time, regarding Hana first and then turning his unwavering eyes on me. I began to feel uncomfortable under his probing stare.

"I admire your spirit, boy," he said at last. "Perhaps I will give you a chance. Come inside, both of you."

He led us through the gateway and into a courtyard shaded by a tall maple tree. Neatly raked sand crunched beneath our feet as we walked. In one corner, a lone student in black *hakama* trousers and a short brown kimono was shuffling and turning swiftly in the dirt, practicing his footwork. A couple of servants were still raking the sand on the courtyard floor. They bowed low when they saw Master Goku, their faces full of respect for him.

"You shall have the opportunity to prove yourselves," the Master said, "but you will not fight any of my students. No." He shook his head, his expression unreadable. "Instead, you will fight me."

I heard Hana gasp, and struggled to hide my own surprise as I bowed to him. "Thank you, sir," I said, barely able to breathe. "We will not disappoint you."

"That remains to be seen," the Master replied. "We will fight hand to hand, and I will test your reflexes, your speed, and your ingenuity. Please remove your swords and sandals."

I swallowed hard. "Now?"

Master Goku nodded. "Immediately," he said. "I see no reason to delay. If you fail to convince me, then it is only fair to give you the rest of the afternoon to make your way to another dojo."

I thought I saw the ghost of a smile curve his lips as he slipped off his sandals and folded back the wide sleeves of his kimono. I remembered my father talking about his own training, many years ago, and how skilled Master Goku was in the art of hand-to-hand combat. He had once defeated ten of his top students, taking them on all at once during an exercise of a simultaneous attack. Ten students! I wondered what Hana and I had let ourselves in for.

But there was no more time to ponder, because my sister and I were both shedding our swords and following Master Goku to the center of the courtyard. As one, we all bowed and assumed a wide-legged stance, knees soft, to show that we were ready. Hana and I mirrored Master Goku, curling one hand into a fist in front of our stomachs while stretching the other arm out in front of our faces, palms flat to the floor and fingertips aimed for our opponent's throat.

Attack first, like the wind, and show him what you

can dô. The thought came to me like a breath of something fresh and pure blown in from the pine forest that surrounded the dojo. . . .

I took a deep breath, emptied my mind of all thought, and attacked.

CHAPTER SEVEN

I took a step forward, then shot out the fist near my stomach hard and fast, aiming straight for Master Goku's chest.

He blocked me with his forearm and before I had time to blink the back of his hand was heading straight for my face. At the same time his other hand was punching toward my stomach, fast and low.

I quickly twisted away, and then hit back with a chop of my own, channeling power from my turn through my arm and into my hand.

Master Goku defended my blow easily, his stance strong and balanced. My next strike was wild and when Goku stepped to the side, I stumbled forward.

Hana darted in. Her outstretched hand swung around and became a chop to Goku's head. Goku deflected it effortlessly and stood with his feet spread wide, knees bent, giving us time to think about our next moves.

Out of the corner of my eye, I saw the lone student

in the corner suddenly dash across the courtyard, the soles of his bare feet flashing white as he disappeared through a carved wooden archway. "Combat in the main courtyard!" he cried. "Come and see!"

Other students took up his excited cry, and soon the words echoed from rooftop to rooftop. As the news spread through the dojo, boys of all ages came jostling through the archway, surrounding us and elbowing one another in order to see.

I tried to ignore the audience and focus on Master Goku and his movements. There was no time to think or feel, but only to act. Limbs moved in a blur. Fists flashed left and right. I struck, blocked, struck again, and sent a hard fist flying. Goku shoved me away, and instantly Hana leaped at him with a high snapping kick. He blocked her and when she landed, he immediately swept her legs out from under her. She broke her fall with a roll that left a track in the sand . . . and for a moment she was out of the fight.

Master Goku spun around to focus on me. He stood firm, totally centered, a towering pillar of strength and calm. I whirled toward him, unleashing one attack after another, trying to keep my hands and feet hard-edged like a steel blade, as my father had taught me. But Master Goku blocked high, then low, then stepped to the side, his movements unhurried, his face tranquil.

Hips twisting, I aimed a furious kick at his stomach. He caught my foot and, with a gentle turn of his wrist, sent me spinning across the sandy courtyard. There was a sharp intake of breath from some of the students as I slapped the ground in a break fall.

Hana recovered herself and abruptly sprang at Master Goku with a sidekick to his knee. He instantly blocked with his shin, spun around, and moved in close to snake his arm over her shoulder. Her balance broken, Hana fell backward and landed in the dirt.

I scrambled to my feet and leaped back into the fight. I launched myself at Master Goku, moving in with one fist pulled back. I showed my intention to punch him, but I planned instead to spin around and hit him with a backward kick. . . .

But the Master was ready. He caught my foot and flipped me flat on my back next to my sister. I gasped, the breath knocked from my body. That had been my best and most agile move—but the Master had anticipated me like a mind reader!

He nodded at us, half smiling as we both lay there in the sand, defeated. A cheer went up from the crowd of students and Master Goku seemed to notice them for the first time.

"You should all be at your studies," he said to them, frowning as he pretended to be displeased. "Knowledge is like a tender plant growing in a garden. What happens if that plant is neglected?"

The students all stood quietly. Then one of them, a pleasant-faced boy with short black hair, spoke up. I recognized him as the student who had been practicing alone when we first came into the courtyard. "A neglected plant will wither and die, Master Goku," he said.

"Indeed it will, Tatsuya." Master Goku acknowledged him with a smile. "Just as a plant withers and dies, so will knowledge slip from your grasp and be forgotten. Go now, all of you, and tend to your studies. You are here to learn, not to stand idle."

The students bowed and hurried away.

Hana and I were still on the floor, but as Master Goku turned back to us, we scrambled to kneel with our shins tucked under our thighs to sit respectfully in *seiza*. My muscles felt weak and I knew I would have bruises the next day.

Master Goku bowed low to us. Together, Hana and I bowed in return, and I remembered what I had said to Ken-ichi earlier about not going onto my knees for anyone. . . .

But Master Goku was different. He was someone who was worth showing respect to.

Master Goku indicated that we should rise and

handed us our swords. We brushed ourselves down and I was aware of him watching us.

I wondered what he was thinking. Did he suspect that we were girls? I stood up straighter and widened my shoulders, trying to look tall and boyish.

Please accept us, I begged silently. I didn't know what I'd do if Master Goku didn't offer us a place in the dojo. We had no other plan.

Master Goku turned to Hana. "Your feet are as light as a gazelle's," he said softly. "Agile, fast, and with a natural grace. What is your name?"

"H—" she began and then stopped, blushing in her confusion. She flashed me a desperate look and my heart began to pound. We hadn't thought of names!

Master Goku smiled encouragingly at her.

Thinking quickly, I spoke up. "Otonashi," I said firmly. "My brother's name is Otonashi. Everyone calls him Silent Fist."

"Otonashi, meaning 'gentle' or 'soundless,'" Master Goku said, gazing at Hana thoughtfully. "A good name. Silence is strength."

He bowed and then moved on to me. "Your focus is strong, my son," he said. "Your kicks are fast and powerful. Does your name also reflect your skill?"

I nodded, inwardly thanking him for the clue, although he of course had no idea he was helping me. "Yes," I said quietly. "My name is Kagenashi and people call me Shadowless Feet."

Master Goku smiled. "You spoke the truth, shadowless one. You both have potential—"

"Oh, thank you!" I cried.

But Master Goku silenced me by raising his hand. "That does not mean I can accept you into my school," he said, a small frown creasing his brow. My heart fell. "I also spoke the truth when I said we have no room. We have just completed the admission of new students for the year. I say that with regret, because I can see your natural talents and I wish I could develop them . . . but I cannot." He bowed again. "I am sorry."

Before we had time to speak, or show our disappointment, Master Goku gestured to one of the nearby servants. "These boys are leaving," he said. "But they've traveled far and are hungry and thirsty. Please fetch them some water and a travel pack of rice so that they can refresh themselves."

The servant nodded and hurried away. I watched him go, my thoughts in turmoil. Master Goku looked at me kindly, and suddenly a new idea broke into my mind like an enormous wave crashing against a cliff. "Servants," I muttered. "We could be servants. . . ."

"Oh yes!" Hana quickly nodded her agreement.

"If your school is full, Master Goku," I went on,

"then there must be much work for your servants. We could help by sweeping the floors and serving food. We could—" I came to an abrupt halt. What else did servants do? Everything! Except that Hana and I had no idea how to do any of it. But the important thing was that we must stay here. We couldn't risk being back out on the road again.

"We're hard workers," I said.

Master Goku folded his hands into his wide sleeves and gazed at me. I wished I could tell what he was thinking.

Eventually he said, "A servant—like a good samurai—must be humble and quiet and patient. Do you have those qualities, Kagenashi?"

I nodded, and beside me Hana nodded too. "We both do," I said firmly.

The servant came hurrying back across the courtyard with a bamboo container and a ball of sticky rice half wrapped in a green leaf. "The food and water, Master," he said.

"Thank you," Master Goku said to the servant. There was a moment's silence and then he added, "I'm sorry to have sent you on a useless errand. These boys have no need for travel food now. They won't be leaving after all."

I caught my breath. "We won't?" I said, grinning. Beside me, Hana's face was shining like the moon on a warm spring night. "We can stay?"

Master Goku smiled. "You can stay," he confirmed. "But I expect hard work from you both. And maybe . . . *maybe* . . . if you work hard enough, you may be rewarded with an invitation to attend some of my classes."

I wanted to leap forward and hug Master Goku, but I knew it would not be polite. And besides, he was already turning away to walk across the courtyard.

"Follow me," he called back over his shoulder. "My servants do not stand idle with grins on their faces when there is work to be done."

Hana and I exchanged delighted glances and then hurried to catch up with the Master as he led us out of the courtyard and along a wooden walkway edged with cherry trees. To our left were buildings and to the right was another small courtyard where four or five students sparred with blunted swords.

"I will introduce you to our head servant here at the dojo," Master Goku said as we turned a corner. Sounds carried up to us from the far corners of the school: the faint thud of an arrow striking a target, a clash of wooden poles, the grunt of someone hitting the ground.

"The head servant's name is Choji," Master Goku

went on. "You will answer to him for everything. He will feed you, clothe you, and give you your orders."

"Yes, Master," Hana and I said together.

We passed a moss garden, then a round pool where a waterfall splashed down from a high rock face. Then, we saw an area of grass where a neat circle of students sat kneeling in *seiza*. They were all staring at a lotus blossom floating in a bowl of water at the center of their circle. A young master in a crisp black jacket and *hakama* trousers walked among them, his face serene.

"Contemplation," Master Goku said, catching my inquiring glance, "can bring serenity and inner tranquillity. Very useful when a warrior is preparing himself for the heat and strife of battle."

I bowed respectfully, grateful that he was teaching us even as we were moving through the school. A sideways glance showed me that Hana was drinking in the sights and sounds, too. I knew that, like me, she would be committing everything to memory. One day, I felt sure we would be grateful for Master Goku's advice.

Eventually we came to a long, low building with a roof that curved upward at each corner. A stocky man in a blue jacket and long breeches appeared in the doorway as we approached. He was thickset, with a neck like a bull, and his hair was shaved on the front part of his head but pulled into the traditional samurai's oiled tail at the back. He carried a bamboo basket full of folded linen, but when he saw Master Goku approaching he put it down and bowed low.

"Ah, Mr. Choji," Master Goku said cheerfully.

"Good afternoon, Sensei," the head servant said, using the traditional term of teacher for the Master. "What can I do for you?"

"I bring you a pair of kitchen boys. This is Otonashi and Kagenashi. I'm sure you'll keep them from idleness."

Choji gave Hana and me a narrow-eyed glance. "They're too skinny," he grumbled. "But I suppose they'll have to do. We're three servants short and I've got to take what I can get!" He picked up his basket of linen. "Now then, skinny boys, I had better show you where you'll sleep. And you'll need clean clothes, too. You're filthy. What have you been doing—drowning yourselves in streams and fighting a path through the forest?"

I bit the inside of my cheeks to stop myself from grinning. Choji had no idea how close to the truth he was!

Master Goku smiled and bowed in our direction. "Today is the first day of *Usui*, or rainwater period, which is a special event for us here at the dojo," he said. "This evening we have a ceremony to mark this official start of a new period of intensive *kenshu* training. There will be plenty of work to do, helping Choji to prepare for the ceremony."

My heart ached as I remembered that this ceremony would have been attended by my father. I had begged to be allowed to accompany him and my brothers—and now karma had brought me here in their place.

Choji was nodding. "Plenty of work to keep you skinny boys busy," he commented brusquely. I began to worry that we might not find the same kindness in Choji that Master Goku had shown us.

"I'll expect to see you both at the ceremony later," Master Goku went on. "You may find it useful to watch the demonstrations of combat. And now, I have my meditation class to attend to. I will leave you in the capable hands of Choji."

With a final bow, Master Goku withdrew, leaving us alone with Choji.

"Come along then, skinny boys," the head servant said, tucking the basket of linen under one of his brawny arms. "I'll show you to your quarters."

We followed him along a hallway, through a sliding door, and into a tiny room with a plain wooden floor. There were rolls of bedding on the shelves and fresh clothes folded in piles.

"Take an extra blanket each from the store cupboard across the hall," Choji said gruffly. "Skinny boys like you must feel the cold."

With a short bow, he left us, sliding the door closed behind him. As I began to peel off my travel-stained clothes, I couldn't help thinking of our bedchamber at home, with its silk hangings, lacquered cabinets, and padded quilts. This tiny, bare room had none of the luxury that we were used to, but it was warm and safe. And if we were to keep our true identities a secret, then Hana and I must not show any sign of discomfort.

We quickly changed into our new blue jackets and baggy breeches. I held my little brother's wooden sword in my hand for a moment, hoping that one day I would hand it back to him and watch the happy smile break across his face. Then I tucked it under my folded-up blanket.

I looked up to see Hana was knotting her sash, and I realized instantly that she was tying it with the knot open to the left.

"No, Hana!" I whispered urgently. "A *lady* ties her sash to the left. A man ties his sash to the *right*."

Hana paused but didn't look at me. For a moment her chin wobbled and I thought she might cry, but no tears fell. Instead she silently untied her sash and retied it with the knot open to the right.

"Hana . . . ?" I said her name gently.

She turned to look at me, her face grave. "My name is Otonashi."

CHAPTER EIGHT

I hugged her. "Okay then, Otonashi," I said, my throat tight. "Let's go and start work."

We found Choji in the kitchens, a square single-story block between the servants' quarters and the largest of the dojo's many practice halls. When we arrived, another young servant boy called Ko was standing at a wooden table chopping vegetables so quickly that his hands seemed to flutter like the wings of a hummingbird. He looked up when we entered and grinned. We grinned back.

Choji turned to see who had come into his kitchen. "Skinny boys!" he ordered. "Come over here. I need someone to taste this soup for me. . . ." He slammed two enormous wooden bowls of fish stew down on the table.

As we made our way across the kitchen, I was aware of Hana swaggering in a boyish way. I adjusted my stride too, taking longer steps and letting my hands swing loosely at my sides.

"Come on—eat up!" Choji urged. "And then tell me what you think. Too much salt? Not enough sugar? What does it need, eh?"

I emptied my bowl with hungry gulps, trying to remember when we'd last eaten. Was it last night, before the *kaiseki ryori*? "This soup is delicious," I told Choji, swiping my cuff across my mouth like a boy. "It needs nothing!"

"Nothing?" Choji barked, and tasted the soup himself. "I'd say it needs more salt. You'd better have some more, so you can taste what I mean." He ladled more soup into our bowls.

After the soup, Choji gave us huge balls of sticky rice and a platter of sweet bamboo shoots to suck on. "If you're going to work here," he said, "I will have to feed you up. I can't have skinny boys in my kitchen— the students might think there's something wrong with my cooking!"

His eyes sparkled as he glanced at me, and because of the extra blankets and bowls of soup, I could see that despite his gruff exterior Choji was a kind man.

When we'd finished eating, he led us to a store-room and gave us our first assignment. "Tonight's opening ceremony is going to be held in the practice hall," he told us. "I want it clean and tidy. Here, boy," he said to Hana. "Sweep and wipe down the wooden floor, then polish it thoroughly with these rags. And take fresh tatami mats and lay them on the raised platform for the Master to sit on."

"And you, Kagenashi," he said, turning to me, "I want you to place these lanterns on their stands all along the walls and light them for when the students assemble at sundown. Then help with the polishing."

I bowed and nodded, my mind reeling. My brothers Nobuaki and Harumasa had often talked about ceremonies at the dojo, describing thrilling demonstrations of combat and skill. But they had never mentioned how much work went into preparing the practice hall! I realized I had never noticed how much work a *kaiseki ryori* ceremony must have been for our household servants.

Choji left us to gather up the mats, lanterns, and their stands, and with an armful each Hana and I hurried across a small garden to the practice hall.

The hall was a huge, airy room, with an ornate roof supported by rows of square pillars. Open gaps along one wall gave a view of the elegant gardens and lily ponds. The enormous wooden floor was dull from repeated footwork practice or body rolls, and we would have to get it gleaming in time for the ceremony.

We spent the rest of the afternoon preparing the

hall. Ko, the young kitchen boy, came to help us.

"I heard you had a fight with Ken-ichi," he said to me as we finished buffing the wooden floorboards. "I hope you got in a few jabs that hurt."

I glanced sideways at him, surprised. For some reason I had thought that my cousin would be popular here at the school. "Don't you like Ken-ichi?" I asked.

Ko shook his head and stood up. "He's a strutting peacock who needs his pride sliced in half with a sharp blade," he said, glancing over his shoulder to make sure nobody else could hear him. "I expect he told you that he's the nephew of the *Jito*? And if he hasn't already, then he soon will! Ken-ichi never lets anyone forget how important he is."

Ko lit three long-handled tapers and handed one each to Hana and me. Together we moved down the hall, lighting the dozens of lanterns that I had hung on their stands. Our shadows began to dance on the walls as we moved back and forth.

"Be wary of Ken-ichi," Ko said, after a while. "He's the kind of boy who bears a grudge. So be on your guard around him, because he's already been grumbling about losing his free hour."

"What could he do to us?" Hana asked quietly.

"He might stick out his foot and trip you when you're hurrying down a walkway with a tray full of tea bowls," Ko said. "And when you look around for someone to blame, he's melted away, leaving you to explain to Choji why all the tea bowls are smashed."

"Has that happened to you?" I asked.

Ko nodded. "Ken-ichi thinks it's hilarious. And Choji thinks I'm clumsy."

"We'll be careful," Hana said.

I nodded. "Thank you for warning us." I knew now that my cousin had changed completely from the boy I had known. Not only had he become arrogant, but he was also cruel.

"That's not all," Ko continued. "Ken-ichi likes to find out every little thing about you, all your secrets, and then use them against you when you're least expecting it."

As Ko reached up to light the last lantern, Hana and I glanced at each other in alarm. If Ken-ichi found out that we were girls, then we'd be finished at the dojo. And if he realized we were hiding from the new *Jito*, we'd be marched to the gates and thrown out into the road, once more at the mercy of Uncle's samurai.

"I don't imagine you two have many secrets, though," Ko said, turning back to us. With a cheerful grin, he blew out his taper. "Come on—we've finished in here. We'd better go back to the kitchens and see what else that old bear Choji wants us to do."

"The head servant seems stern," Hana murmured.

"That's just part of his act," Ko told her. "The only time he ever really gets mad is if we don't do our work!"

We were busy for the rest of the afternoon: raking the gravel pathway that led through the garden to the practice hall, sweeping the floor in the kitchen, and polishing dozens of eating bowls and tea bowls, stacking them on black-and-red-lacquered trays ready for the ceremony. Exhausted, Hana and I struggled on. Our backs ached and our hands and feet were blistered from work we weren't accustomed to.

The sun was just slipping behind the curving red rooftops of the dojo when Choji told us to gather up our laden trays and follow him back across to the practice hall.

When we stepped inside, I caught my breath. The high-ceilinged hall was crowded and buzzing, filled with a warm golden light. Row upon row of students sat on small round cushions on the wooden floor. Some were much older than us, calm and serious-looking, their dark brown sashes showing their seniority. Others were much younger, with white sashes and open, friendly faces. They sat in orderly rows around the edges of the hall, talking quietly. Dotted among them were a handful of young masters in their black jackets and *hakama* trousers.

I caught sight of Ken-ichi and his two friends. When he saw me, Ken-ichi shot me a look of surprise, which turned into a sneer when he took in my blue servant's uniform and the black-lacquered tray in my hands.

Ignoring him, I followed Ko and Hana. I couldn't worry about Ken-ichi because acting like a servant was taking up all of my concentration. I tried to remember the way the maids at home had been almost invisible at times, moving silently and unobtrusively through our compound, making sure our lives had been easy and comfortable.

Choji raised his hand in some kind of signal. My heart thumped because I didn't know what he meant and I exchanged an anxious glance with Hana. Were we going to give ourselves away so soon? But then the other servants began to move among the students and young masters, kneeling to serve tea. Immediately Hana and I hurried to copy them.

A few of the students glanced expectantly at the raised platform at the far end of the room, and moments later, Master Goku swept in and took his place there. He looked even more impressive than when I had first seen him at the gates, and the atmosphere in the room seemed more energized once he arrived.

He bowed to his students, his ceremonial robes rippling. He wore a long kimono, its shimmering silk like a rushing blue waterfall beneath an over-robe of the darkest green with elaborate stiffened shoulders. His long gray hair had been smoothed, plaited, and then coiled on the crown of his head in the way I had seen my father's styled when he was visiting the *bakufu* in Kamakura or the Imperial Court in Kyoto. He carried two ornate swords on his left side, showing his status as master and samurai.

"I am honored to welcome you all to the ceremony that opens *kenshu*," Master Goku said, "our period of intensive training." His deep voice was soft and almost musical, but it carried to the far corners of the large hall with ease. "I know that the older students among you will be surprised to see me standing alone on this platform. After all, it is customary for our great Lord Steward, the *Jito*, to begin our ceremony. Sadly, however, Lord Yoshijiro cannot be with us tonight."

When I heard my father's name, my heart jumped in shock and I almost spilled the tea I was pouring.

Taking a deep breath to calm myself, I sat back on my heels to look around the hall for Hana. She stood motionless a few paces away, her lacquered tray held stiffly in front of her. She was staring at Master Goku like a lifeless statue.

I got up and hurried to her side, stepping quietly so as not to draw attention to my movements. I nodded purposefully at her tray, and then slowly and deliberately kneeled to serve tea to the nearest student.

Hana seemed to gather herself together. She moved silently along the row, kneeled, and poured tea just as before.

Master Goku was still speaking. I tried to concentrate on what he was saying as I carried on with my duties.

"I received a message yesterday morning explaining that Lord Yoshijiro was unable to attend our ceremony," he continued. "An emergency has taken him to another part of the province, and he will not return in time for tonight's event."

Yesterday morning! He had received a message yesterday morning? I realized with horror that Uncle must have cancelled on his behalf—in *advance* of the murder the night before!

I felt a chill settle around my heart at the thought of Uncle's cold-blooded plotting. I tried to remember whether there had been any change in him, perhaps some hint that his betrayal was coming.

He had always seemed so close to my father, and yet all the time he must have been nursing a deep and bitter resentment. More than resentment— hatred! Uncle . . . of all people. I despaired as I remembered his laughter, his many kindnesses, the way he had always pinched my cheek so affectionately.

But then I had a sudden glancing memory of another side to Uncle Hidehira. Like the day he had flared up at Ken-ichi for accidentally breaking a tea bowl or the time I had seen him whipping a man-servant for lack of respect.

How long had he been planning to murder my family?

"I have sent a messenger back to the *Jito*," Master Goku went on, "inviting him to visit us upon his return. I am sure that he will come here to the dojo very soon, to see how his loyal samurai students are progressing."

It was clear that Master Goku didn't know of Father's death. I swallowed hard as I wondered what information the messenger would bring back to the dojo. What were Uncle's plans? Surely he could not hide the burned-down buildings of the *Jito*'s home. What would he tell Master Goku?

"Lord Yoshijiro sends his best wishes," Master Goku said, "and tells us to look forward to the future.

And it is indeed the future that concerns us all tonight."

The future? I thought bitterly, seeing the hidden message from Uncle within the words that had been sent to Master Goku. *The future is Uncle as* Jito.

Master Goku's robes rippled as he took a step forward, closer to the edge of the platform. "As many of you are aware, we are about to enter a new regime of training. This intensive *kenshu* will end as usual with the annual tournament on the bright and clear first day of the *Seimei* period, more than forty days from now."

At the mention of an annual tournament, the atmosphere in the hall became charged with excitement. Boys shifted and nudged each other.

"For those of you who do not know," the Master said, "the tournament is a great event in the school calendar. Each year we throw open the gates of the dojo and people come from far and wide across the province to watch as students of all grades and experience pit themselves against each other. From nobles' sons to servants, anyone can compete."

Hana and I passed each other midway along a row of students, and she raised her eyebrows as if to say, *Anyone can compete . . . that means us.* But I shook my head. We had to stay beneath notice, make sure that we stayed hidden. If we were lucky,

Uncle's men might give up looking for us soon. I didn't know how long we could stay at the dojo, but I knew we couldn't do anything to draw attention to ourselves.

Up on the platform, Master Goku was explaining how the tournament would proceed.

"By the end of the day, one student will emerge as our champion," he said. "And we will honor him, because he will have proved himself to be the most gifted student in this dojo and worthy of the title of samurai."

A flutter of applause and cheering went up, and Master Goku smiled. "I must remind you all, however, that the tournament is not about glory. It is about honor, courage, and self-discipline. Champions are not born, they are made . . . and every boy in this school has it within him to become champion."

I kneeled to serve Ken-ichi and his two friends, holding my sleeve back and pouring with as much grace as I could.

Ken-ichi watched me with a sneer on his face. "What did you say about kneeling to no one, rice boy?" he hissed. "Isn't that what you said just before I defeated you?"

I flushed with anger, but I remembered Goku's words to Ken-ichi about controlling his pride and didn't respond. Determined to follow the

Master's advice, I finished pouring for Ken-ichi and moved on.

When everyone had been served tea, I returned to Choji, along with Hana and Ko. We waited silently for our next orders.

Master Goku's dark gaze swept the hall as he spoke, seeming to take in every face. "You are all here because you have been chosen," he said. "I have watched each of you fight and selected you because you each possess a core of inner strength. And it is my belief that each and every one of you can be a champion. Work hard. Keep your focus. Allow determination and passion to burn within you, and you will be rewarded with success."

A ripple of anticipation went through the students. Looks of sturdy determination appeared on the faces of the older boys while a few of the younger ones began to whisper eagerly to each other. I saw Ken-ichi exchange a glance with one of his friends. A smile of superiority curved across my cousin's lips, as though he had already decided that *he* would be champion. I gritted my teeth, hoping with all my heart that Ken-ichi would not succeed. If he did, his vanity and arrogance would be unbearable!

The students were still chattering, and as the level of noise rose in the hall, Master Goku smiled and held up his hands for silence. "Enough with words!" he cried. "Let us see *action*. I declare the *kenshu* open . . . and may the demonstrations commence!"

Immediately the hall took on an atmosphere of expectation as a pair of young warriors in full combat dress sprang onto the central practice mat. One was a short, stocky boy with a face as round as a pumpkin, the other had bushy eyebrows that reminded me of caterpillars. They bowed to Master Goku on his platform and then to each other, their faces composed. Then they leaped into action, arms poised and legs kicking high. I could see that both were skilled, and I found myself studying their moves carefully, hoping to learn what I could from them.

After several minutes of sparring, it was clear that the boy with the bushy eyebrows was the victor. Cheers rose from the assembled students as he bowed and accepted a word of praise from Master Goku.

At a whispered instruction from Choji, Hana and I hurried out to the center of the hall to wipe down the floorboards that may have been scuffed during the combat. Afterward we swiftly made our way back to the head servant and waited for the next demonstration.

A pair of combatants came in carrying *jo*. They

sparred elegantly with the long, straight wooden poles, but with a deadly ferocity that stole my breath. When they had finished, four of the younger students dashed into the ring and displayed the twelve movements of the *kata*. Their small faces were taut with concentration as they moved slowly and gracefully, striving hard to please the Master. At the end of their bout, they stood in a perfect line and bowed low, their faces pink with pleasure as the applause rang out.

"You must help with the next demonstration," Choji whispered to Hana and me. "Set up the archery target!" and he pointed to the far wall.

We had just returned to our places at the edge of the room when Hana nudged me. A student was making his way through the crowded room. I recognized him as the boy who had been practicing alone in the outer courtyard when we had first arrived at the dojo. He was bright faced, cheerful-looking, and I guessed that he was about my age. He was holding an elegant longbow as he stepped confidently into the mat area.

"Tatsuya?" I heard Ken-ichi scoff at the boy's name, just loud enough so Tatsuya could hear. "Why is that peasant doing a demonstration?"

Tatsuya blushed but ignored Ken-ichi's taunt. He took his place in front of the archery target, bowed to Master Goku, and fitted an arrow to his longbow. Everyone fell silent as he took stock of the target, eyes narrowed. Then he turned and strode to the far end of the hall.

Slowly Tatsuya raised his longbow until the arrow was level with his nose. Elbow high, he drew back the strings and took aim. The longbow flexed, its supple length curving backward. Abruptly Tatsuya loosed his arrow. It sliced through the air, straight and true, piercing the target dead center.

Almost before the first arrow had hit, Tatsuya was loosing a second, and then a third. The second arrow split the first straight down the middle of the shaft to embed itself in the same spot at the center of the target. The third split the second, so that all three arrows were held in the same hole.

I gasped, impressed. Tatsuya beckoned to Hana and she leaped to her feet. He pointed to a tall, thin paper screen that stood against the wall near the target.

"Would you bring that forward, please?" he asked her with a friendly smile. "Position it so that I cannot see the target."

Hana did as he asked, and the two bowed to each other before she returned to her place beside me.

Tatsuya's face was blank, his eyes dark and unreadable as he stared at the paper screen. Then he fitted a fourth arrow to his longbow, took aim, and loosed . . .

The arrow whistled as it flew through the air, cleanly piercing the screen with a neat hole and hitting the target with a thud.

There was silence in the hall as Hana hurried to remove the paper screen. Immediately everyone in the room could see that Tatsuya had speared the three previous arrows with this fourth—and hit the center of the target with almost impossible accuracy.

The students burst into wild applause and some of the younger boys shouted out encouragement. I noticed that Ken-ichi was not applauding, his face set in a hard frown. His jealousy of Tatsuya was obvious.

Master Goku smiled. "A perfect demonstration of all that can be achieved with self-discipline, tenacity, and long hours of practice," he said. "Despite your humble beginnings, Tatsuya, you have the makings of a warrior of the finest class."

Choji beckoned us back, and as Hana and I threaded our way between the rows of students I saw that Ken-ichi's face was so sour it looked as if he had sucked the juice from a whole barrel full of citron fruit. He caught my gaze and jerked his chin up.

As I drew level with him, he shot his foot out and

caught me hard across the front of my ankles.

His movement was so swift that I did not have time to take evasive action. I pitched forward like a felled tree, arms outstretched. I knocked against another student and spilled his bowl of tea into his lap.

The student leaped to his feet. "Watch out!" he cried angrily. "Clumsy idiot."

Everyone in the hall turned to see what the commotion was about. Master Goku was frowning, an expression of displeasure on his usually tranquil face. I scrambled to my feet in time to see a furious-looking Choji bearing down on me.

"I'm so sorry," I said to Choji through gritted teeth. I was furious with myself for not remembering Ko's earlier warning about Ken-ichi's habit of tripping servants. I had just ruined my plan for not drawing attention to myself. "It was an accident."

"Accident or not, you will apologize to this student," Choji said tightly.

I bowed low. "My humble apologies," I said sincerely.

The student gave me a curt bow and Choji pulled me off to the side of the mat.

"You must be more careful, Kagenashi," he said in a stern voice. "We must never disturb the students in their learning. Do you understand me?"

"Yes, Choji," I said meekly.

As Choji stared down at me, his gaze hard, I silently prayed that his kindness would stop him short of throwing me out of the dojo.

"Let there be no repeat of this clumsiness," he said at last.

"No, Choji." I bowed.

As the head servant turned away from me, I caught a last glimpse of Ken-ichi. He looked so pleased with himself that it took all my self-control to stop myself from leaping at him and punching the smirk off his face.

CHAPTER NINE

After the demonstrations, the ceremony continued with a feast. At a gruff word from Choji, Hana and the other servants hurried to bring long, low tables.

I glanced at the head servant and he gave me a curt nod. "You, too. But be careful. I'll be watching you."

We positioned the tables and began to serve food. The students gathered around, kneeling and helping themselves eagerly to balls of sticky rice, rolled seaweed, and platters of fish that had been crisped on a hot griddle.

At Ken-ichi's table, I noticed that my cousin was sitting beside Tatsuya, who was holding his longbow across his lap. They were talking quietly, their dark heads bent together.

As I served rice and fish nearby, I strained my ears to hear what Ken-ichi was saying.

" . . . and ceremony also demands that we never

109

use our *hashi* chopsticks to point, or to share food with another student," Ken-ichi told him. "To use your *hashi* like that would be most impolite."

"Thank you, Ken-ichi," Tatsuya said. "I'm grateful that you're taking the time to tell me these things. It's so difficult to remember all the rules, and I'm terrified of offending Master Goku in some way."

"I don't suppose you learned such things as etiquette, growing up in the rice fields as you did," Ken-ichi said.

I glanced sharply at my cousin, but there was no trace of mockery on his face. He looked serious and concerned, as if he really was trying to be kind and helpful. Tatsuya seemed to have been taken in, despite Ken-ichi's earlier taunting, but I was suspicious of my cousin. He was up to something—but what?

I decided to keep an eye on him as I went about my duties. I carried trays and bowls to the young masters, served more tea, and hurried back and forth between the hall and the kitchens. But Ken-ichi carried on being friendly and attentive to Tatsuya.

"You're a good friend, Ken-ichi," I heard Tatsuya say. "Coming here to this school has made me realize how little I know about the rules of society."

"You'll learn," Ken-ichi told him with an easy smile.

"Just stick with me, Tatsuya, and you'll be fine."

I wanted to speak out—to warn Tatsuya that it wasn't true. But I could feel the head servant's gaze on me and I knew I couldn't risk getting into trouble for disturbing the students again.

The ceremony and feasting had gone on so long that some of the lanterns had gone out. Conversation filled the room and fireflies danced above the heads of some of the students and masters as they chattered. Choji handed each servant a large ornate bamboo fan and told us to take up places among the students. We were to stir the air above their heads and keep them cool as they relaxed after the feast.

I quickly whispered to Hana, and together we made our way to Ken-ichi's table. I was determined that if my cousin made a move, I would be there to stop him.

At last, Master Goku held up a hand for silence. He was still sitting in formal style on a tatami mat up on the platform. A couple of the other young masters had joined him during the feast.

"We have gathered here as students, teachers, and friends," Master Goku said. "We've seen demonstrations of great combat and skill that seem almost magical. But remember that inside each and every one of you beats the heart of a warrior. Magic is merely practice and discipline." He smiled serenely and bowed his head. "And now—I will bid you good night."

I noticed Ken-ichi whispering to Tatsuya but I couldn't make out what he was saying. Then, Tatsuya began to stand up.

My heart skipped a beat. On such a formal occasion as this, rising before the Master showed a terrible lack of manners. Master Goku would be insulted—and Tatsuya would be completely shamed. I couldn't think how to stop him, until Hana nudged me and motioned stepping down with her foot.

Quickly realizing what she meant, I deliberately placed my foot on the back of Tatsuya's kimono, making it impossible for him to stand up. He wobbled, and furiously whipped around to glare at Hana and me. I pressed my finger to my lips and shook my head, trying to warn him with my eyes. I hoped Choji hadn't noticed anything out of the ordinary.

Then, up on the raised platform, Master Goku was on his feet. Tatsuya turned back just in time to see the Master gesture to the rest of the school, his hands spread wide, palms upward. I released Tatsuya's kimono.

In a heartbeat, every student and master in the hall were on their feet, including Tatsuya. He shot Ken-ichi an accusing look as he realized what had almost happened. But my cousin's cruel smile showed no remorse.

As Tatsuya half turned to give me an almost imperceptible bow of thanks, Ken-ichi looked sharply at me, but I avoided his gaze.

All around us, the students parted to make a pathway for Master Goku as he swept down from the platform and made his way toward the doorway. As he drew level with me, his dark gaze slid to my face, and he regarded me for a brief moment. There was curiosity in his glance and I wondered whether he had noticed what I had done.

Then the moment was over. Master Goku had left the room and disappeared into the night. I could breathe again.

"Get moving, slave!" Ken-ichi snapped, glaring at me. I guessed that he knew I was the reason his trick with Tatsuya had failed. "You're not supposed to stop fanning us until the hall is empty!"

Normally I would have reacted angrily, but this time I knew I had scored a victory over Ken-ichi. I smiled sweetly at him and bowed low.

Ken-ichi seethed. A moment later he was gone, roughly shouldering past me with his friends at his heels.

Later, back in our room, we whispered about the events of the evening as we got ready for bed.

"Ken-ichi is even worse than I thought," Hana said, loosening her hair from her topknot and combing it with her fingers. "I'm so glad you stopped Tatsuya from shaming himself."

"Me, too," I agreed. "He seems nice. And I've never seen anyone use a longbow with such accuracy!"

"I've never seen anyone who knows as much as Master Goku does," Hana said, shaking her head. "He knew you'd helped Tatsuya."

"He doesn't miss a thing, does he?" I agreed. "We'll have to be very careful when we're around him. If he finds out that we've lied to him . . . that we're not who we say we are . . ."

Hana looked troubled.

"Don't worry," I said firmly, as we shook out our bedding rolls and climbed into bed, arranging the thin covers, and the extra blankets that Choji had offered, around us. I was so tired that I hardly noticed they weren't the soft, silk-covered quilts I had enjoyed at home. "We've convinced everyone that we're boys. Now all we have to do is make sure that even *we* forget that we're girls. Then we won't put a foot wrong, and everything will be fine."

Hana seemed to accept that, and very soon she was asleep, worn out by the events of the past two days. I stayed awake longer, lying with my arms

114

tucked beneath my head. The paper screens had a small gap between them and for a while I watched ragged clouds drift across the face of the moon.

It had been only a day since our father and brothers had been taken from us. Our home, too. My sister and I had killed a man—a samurai! And now we were servants in a samurai training school, disguised as boys, under the watchful eye of Master Goku. We were safe, for now, and I offered up a prayer that Mother and Moriyasu would also be kept safe until we could all be together again.

Just before I slipped into a fitful sleep, I vowed to myself that I would do everything I could to please Master Goku, so that he might teach me the skills of a samurai.

And once I had become a warrior, my uncle would never be able to hurt my family again.

The next morning Hana and I were up before dawn, woken by a harsh knocking on the door frame and Choji's voice. "Come on, skinny boys!" he cried. "The kitchen chores are waiting."

"I hardly slept a wink," I grumbled to Hana as we pulled on our jackets and breeches. "I ache all over from our fight with Master Goku yesterday."

"And from all the serving," Hana said. "The sleeping mats are so thin. I'd give anything to have my lovely futon bed from home, covered in a pile of soft feather quilts!"

We hurried to the kitchens, where we found that our first job of the day was to help Ko and Choji serve breakfast to the students and masters. When they had all eaten and hurried away to their lessons, Choji thrust bowls of sweet rice into our hands. "Eat," he commanded. "And then it will be time to clean the bedchambers."

When we had eaten, Ko hurried to clear away the bowls and Choji ordered me to make tea for everyone. I nodded and hurried across the kitchen to hang the large pot over the bright charcoal brazier. Making tea was something I had done for my mother and father many times, and I felt a lilt of happy confidence as I took the lid off a big black teapot.

"Here's the tea," Ko said helpfully, lifting a bamboo box down from a high shelf and handing it to me.

"Thank you." I heaped green leaves into the pot, trying to work out how many scoops I would need for everyone. There were ten servants, and Choji, and Hana and me—

"What are you doing?" Ko grabbed my wrist. "You're using far too much tea." He peered into the pot for a moment and then glanced up at me in astonishment. "Only the Emperor himself could afford to use all that!"

I froze, panic-stricken.

"I . . . I . . ." I swallowed hard, my mind almost a blank. *Think, Kimi!* "Our last master was quite wealthy," I stuttered at last.

"Wealthy?" Ko said, giving me a strange look. "Your last master must have been the *Jito* himself. Us ordinary mortals can only afford one scoop of tea."

I bit my lip as I realized how different life was here. One scoop, for so many people? I was beginning to understand how privileged Hana and I had been.

Luckily no one else seemed to have noticed anything, and the rest of the meal passed without incident. Soon Hana and I were on our way to clean the students' bedchambers, armed with brooms and dusters.

The first room we were assigned to was Ken-ichi's. He was still there, rifling through piles of discarded kimonos as he searched for his *bokken*. When he saw us, he shot us a filthy look and deliberately kicked over a half-full bowl of bean curd soup. The brown liquid seeped across the floor and began to soak into one of the bedsheets.

"Clean that up, rice boy," he snarled. "I want this

117

room spotless by the time I get back. If it isn't, I'll complain to Master Goku. He saw you throw tea into that student's lap last night, so he already thinks you're clumsy. And once I tell him you spilled soup in my room, I guarantee you'll be out of the dojo by midday." With that, Ken-ichi snatched up his *bokken* and swaggered off down the hallway.

Hana and I watched him for a moment, and then Hana shrugged and got down on her knees to mop up the mess.

"I'll do that," I said. "It's me he hates, not you."

"We'll both do it," Hana replied quietly. "He's my cousin, too."

We mopped up the soup, and then attacked the rest of the room—flinging open the shutters and shaking out bedding as we had seen our own servants do at home. I struggled with a discarded kimono for a while, trying to remember how my own had been folded. Were the arms folded inward, or behind . . . ? At last it looked right, and all the kimonos were put tidily away in a cupboard.

"Remember how we used to play games with the maids while they were dusting?" Hana asked me as she went over the floor with a damp cloth.

"I'm glad we did," I said with a nod, reaching up with a leafy bamboo pole to hook fine cobwebs from the corners of the ceiling. "Otherwise we wouldn't have a clue what to do now."

Eventually we were finished.

"I hope every room isn't going to take us this long," I muttered.

The next bedchamber was so neat that at first I thought it must be a spare room. But then I saw a student sitting in *seiza*, head bowed and eyes closed. It was Tatsuya, and he was meditating.

Horrified at having almost disturbed him, I began to back out, but I backed into Hana who protested and Tatsuya's eyes flashed open. He stared at us in surprise.

"My apologies," I said, bowing deeply. "I didn't realize any of the students were in their rooms."

"Please come in." With a friendly smile, Tatsuya scrambled to his feet and beckoned Hana and me into his room. His brown kimono was fastened with a white sash and black breeches that stopped just below the knee. "I was hoping to see you today."

"You—you were?"

"I wanted to thank you for what you did at the feast last night." He spoke slowly, haltingly, as if he wasn't used to using such a formal way of speaking. "If you had not stepped on the back of my kimono, I would have risen before the Master and disgraced myself."

"It was Ha—" I caught myself just in time. "Not

119

me—but my brother who saved you," I finished, stumbling a little over the word *brother* as I drew Hana forward. "He noticed, and nudged me. I just did what anyone would have done."

"Then I am indebted to you both." Tatsuya bowed low. "If there's anything I can do for either of you— you have only to ask."

We bowed and returned to our cleaning. Tatsuya picked up his longbow and began to tighten the string, his hands quick and confident. I remembered his demonstration last night, his skill and accuracy, and suddenly an idea came to me.

"Tatsuya," I said hesitantly. "Maybe there is something you can do for us. . . ."

He glanced up at me, smiling. "What?"

"Would you . . ." I hesitated again, afraid that he would dismiss my request. After all, he was a student while Hana and I were just lowly servants. But Tatsuya's smile and bright, friendly eyes gave me confidence. "My brother and I would like to train, as well as work as servants. It would be good for us to practice with a student as skilled as you are. Would you spar with us sometimes?"

"I would be happy to," he said, hanging his bow back up on the wall next to a *jo* pole. "I'm always ready for extra practice." He glanced at Hana, and then looked back at me. "What are your names?"

"I am Otonashi," Hana said.

"I'm Kagenashi," I added.

"Well, my new friends," Tatsuya said. "When it comes to sparring, my father always used to say that there's no time like the present!" He quickly snatched his *jo* down from its hook on the wall, sweeping it around in an elegant curve.

He took me by surprise, slicing into an attack almost before I had time to raise the broom I was carrying. But I deflected the *jo* with the broom handle, twisted, and immediately Tatsuya and I were circling each other, watching to see who would make the next move. My broom handle was about the same length as Tatsuya's *jo*, and I hoped it would prove as sturdy.

His gaze still fixed on me, Tatsuya suddenly launched a sideways attack on Hana. She ducked quickly and darted behind Tatsuya, trying to catch one end of his *jo* with her dusting cloth, wrapping it and pulling it down. She was graceful even in the smallest of her movements.

The three of us danced back and forth across the room, sidestepping bedding rolls. The room echoed to the sound of wooden poles clashing together.

I soon found myself out of breath, and Tatsuya was sweating. "You're both very good," he acknowledged. "Next time I'll remember to take on only one of you at a time!"

I grinned and whipped a wide arc with my broom,

catching his weapon and trapping it for a moment. Tatsuya broke free and raised the weapon to strike from above. I twisted my body, spinning myself out of reach of his *jo*, turning toward the open doorway—

Where I froze.

We were being watched—by Master Goku!

CHAPTER TEN

Immediately I flipped my broom up the right way. Beside me, Tatsuya slid into a perfect *kata* practice stance while Hana dropped to her knees and began to rub at an invisible stain on the floor.

But we didn't fool Master Goku for a moment. He took a step into the bedchamber and gently took hold of my broom. "Your moves show promise," he said. "But perhaps you'll allow me to demonstrate a more correct technique?"

I glanced up at him from beneath my lashes and saw that his eyes sparkled good-naturedly as he twisted the length of wood and showed me a firm two-handed grip.

"You need to keep the weapon steady," he told the three of us. "And use it to gain control over your opponent. Tatsuya, attack me." Tatsuya did not hesitate and moved to strike Goku from above. Goku raised the broom to protect his head from the strike and, in the same movement, twisted the long stick around Tatsuya's. Moving his weapon in a tight downward spiral, Goku dropped to his knees and trapped Tatsuya's *jo* against the floor.

"Thank you, Sensei," I said humbly, and bowed as Goku handed the broom back to me. "I will remember that."

Master Goku gazed thoughtfully at Hana and me. "I observed you both during the *kenshu* ceremony yesterday," he said. "And I was pleased with what I saw. Perhaps you would both like to attend a study class in the scroll room later this morning?"

Hana and I exchanged astounded glances.

"We would be honored to!" I exclaimed.

"You have earned the right to be there," Master Goku said lightly.

With a small bow he turned and left the room, leaving me wondering what he had meant. What had he seen that pleased him? Our work as servants or what happened with Tatsuya?

But it didn't matter why we had been chosen. It was enough to know that we had pleased Master Goku. Hana and I were going to begin our studies under a *real* master. Our skills would improve and grow, helping us to become strong enough to take revenge on our uncle.

We thanked Tatsuya for sparring with us and he

went to his next class, leaving us to finish our cleaning. As Hana and I quickly worked through our chores, I thought about the study class we would attend later. I was excited and grateful that we had been invited to the scroll room, but secretly my heart longed for Goku to allow us into one of his training classes, where we could run and kick and twist and leap!

After Choji dismissed us, we hurried along a covered walkway to the scroll room and saw immediately that we were the last to arrive. The other students were already kneeling at the low tables that were grouped around the center of the room, their colored sashes a kaleidoscope of orange, green, and blue. They were copying a scroll that hung at the front of the room.

The scroll room was light and airy, the size of ten or twelve tatami. The screens had been opened onto a garden full of lush green foliage. Master Goku was bent forward over his own table in the middle, studying a long scroll covered in flowing black *kanji* characters.

He looked up as Hana and I entered. "Come and take your places," he said with a warm smile. "There is a table at the back you may share. I have put out brushes and scrolls for you—they are well used but still serviceable, I believe."

As we made our way across the classroom, Master Goku turned to the other students. "Although these boys are wearing servants' uniforms, you will treat them both with respect and humility. During training, all boys are equal. Everyone, whether student or servant, has something to learn . . . and something to contribute. Now, please continue your copying."

The other students went back to their work as Hana and I took our places. Ken-ichi was sitting at the table next to ours. I was surprised to see him looking happy and relaxed, almost his old self. But then he glanced up and caught my eye. Immediately his shoulders tensed and he scowled. I quickly looked away and moved on.

Just behind Ken-ichi was Tatsuya. We smiled at each other, and I knew that Hana and I had at least one friend in the room.

Kneeling at the table, Hana reached for an ink brush eagerly. I quickly poured some water onto the ink stone, and dabbed the dried ink stick into the little pool of liquid, turning it black. I selected another of the brushes, dipped the tip into the wet ink and swept it back and forth across the ink stone until it was coated with thick charcoal ink. As Master Goku had said, the brushes were well-used and most of the scrolls were already covered with faded *kanji* characters.

No matter. My fresh black ink will show up over the faded gray, I thought as I began my first stroke. I knew Hana and I were lucky that Master Goku had provided for us when we could not provide for ourselves. I hoped that one day we would be able to repay his kindness.

Beside me, Hana drew her brush downward in a graceful sweep, like water flowing over a smooth rock. At the end of the stroke, she lifted the tip of her brush clear of the paper, and then made another curving movement. As she covered her scroll in elegant *kanji*, I saw that her face looked tranquil for the first time since we had fled from the compound. She seemed at peace.

In contrast to Hana's writing, my own *kanji* seemed awkward and choppy. I could not find a rhythm, and as the black ink spread downward over the paper like the waves of a rough sea, I imagined my mother standing at my shoulder, shaking her head in disappointment.

"Ah, Kimi, my dearest daughter," she would say. "You are so much like your father. It is such a shame you do not apply the same focus to elegant writing as you do your sword skills."

For a moment, her presence seemed so strong that I imagined I could smell her cherry blossom perfume. But then I realized it was merely a hint of incense, carried in on a light breeze through the gap in the screens. My throat went tight and I blinked as I tried to concentrate on applying the correct pressure for each stroke of my *kanji*.

Master Goku had begun to walk slowly around the room, stopping to correct the way a student held a brush or to give advice on the way characters should be spaced on the scrolls.

"You may wonder why writing is so important to a samurai," he said in his quiet, firm voice. "Of course, the importance of reading is obvious. How else can a man read the poems of the masters and gain greater understanding of the path a warrior must tread? And how else can a warrior follow instructions if he cannot read dispatches from his general who may be on the far side of a battlefield?" The Master paused by one of the gaps in the screens and gazed serenely around the room. "But writing . . . why is writing important? Perhaps one of our older students might enlighten the new boys?"

One of Ken-ichi's friends raised his hand and Master Goku smiled at him. "Please go ahead."

"We learned last year that writing promotes inner strength," the boy said. "The literary arts are as important to samurai as martial arts."

"Indeed, that is so," Master Goku said, folding his hands into the wide sleeves of his robe as he moved around the room once more. "Literary arts and martial arts are like the two wheels of a carriage. They keep everything in balance. Can you expand upon that theme, Ken-ichi?"

"Yes, Sensei," Ken-ichi responded. "You have taught us that creating beauty in our writing brings serenity and inner tranquillity, in much the same way as contemplation of a beautiful painting or a cleverly designed garden."

Master Goku smiled. "Well done, Ken-ichi. A serene mind will triumph over a troubled mind, just as composed movements will defeat erratic ones."

I bent my head over my work and tried to focus on my own inner tranquillity, covering my scroll in thick black strokes. Master Goku paused as he came to our table and watched Hana as she conjured a series of sweeping characters that reminded me of weeping willow trees.

She glanced up at him when she had finished and he nodded. "Beautiful," he said. "You write with grace and with a nobility that is rare in one of your status."

Hana lowered her gaze modestly, but my heart was beating slightly faster than before. *Nobility* . . . once again my sister and I were in danger of giving away our true status by our tiniest actions.

I swallowed hard and twisted my wrist, making my next stroke even more awkward and harsh looking.

Master Goku sighed when he came to inspect my progress. "Short strokes require quick and even pressure," he said. "Try to imitate the curve of a swan's neck. . . ."

As the Master moved away, I glanced up to see Ken-ichi smirking at me. "Just face the fact that you're a peasant, rice boy, and peasants have no use for writing."

Master Goku suddenly loomed over Ken-ichi's shoulder. "You could improve the refinement of your stroke if you concentrated more on yourself rather than those around you, Ken-ichi," he said quietly.

Ken-ichi flushed deep red. "Yes, Sensei."

I couldn't help feeling a tiny dab of pleasure at his embarrassment. Master Goku gave him a stern look before moving on. We all bent our heads to our work, and for the remainder of the morning the lesson was conducted in near silence. The only sound was the sweep of sable brushes on paper.

When Master Goku finally dismissed us, we all filed quietly past him, placing our scrolls onto his table. I was last in line. As I drew level with the Master, he reached out and took my scroll straight from my hand before I had time to put it with all the rest. Unfurling it, he studied the poem I had copied from one of the scrolls hanging on the wall at the back of the classroom.

"Where did you learn to write, Kagenashi?" he asked.

My mind raced as I considered the possibilities. Where *would* a peasant have learned to write? I glanced at Hana who was standing by the door. Her wide eyes showed her concern, but there was no way for her to help me.

Master Goku, meanwhile, was waiting patiently for my answer.

"In her youth, my grandmother lived with the servants of the *Jito*'s family," I blurted at last. "She learned to write there. Sometimes when it was too cold to venture out, she would give lessons to my brother and me."

Hana nodded to confirm my story, and I could see that she was glad I had managed not to lie outright to our teacher. Grandmother had often given us extra writing lessons when the weather kept us from practicing outside, and she *did* live with the *Jito*'s servants, but not as one of them as I had implied.

"Then your grandmother was a skilled tutor. The characters she taught you have great refinement." Master Goku looked up at Hana and me. I could not read the expression in his eyes. "Long ago, I taught a student who formed his *kanji* in much the same way as you do," he continued. "Firm pressure on the downstrokes . . . a certain choppiness in the upward sweeps . . . the brush wielded as if it were a sword . . ."

His next words sent my heart fluttering. "If someone else had brought me this scroll," he said quietly, "and they did not tell me where it had come from, I would have said that this writing came from the brush of the great *Jito* himself, Lord Steward Yoshijiro."

I stared in horror at the Master. Had he guessed our secret?

CHAPTER ELEVEN

"My grandmother would be honored to hear you say such a thing," I said, trying to keep my voice level.

"I would like to meet your grandmother one day," Master Goku said.

"Alas, Sensei, she is dead," I told him. "Two winters ago, a sickness came and took many souls, including my grandmother's." I remembered the sad day of Grandmother's funeral so well. The weather had been bitterly cold and an icy wind seemed to freeze our tears. That was the only time I ever saw my father cry.

"I'm sorry to hear that." Master Goku gently placed my scroll with all the others. "I feel she and I would have had much to talk about. She must have known the *Jito* when he was a young man, as I did."

"Y-you knew the *Jito*?" I asked, pretending ignorance.

"Lord Yoshijiro studied here many years ago,"

Master Goku said. "He was a remarkable student. Very skilled. Born to be a warrior and a leader of men."

My heart twisted as I thought of my father, the way I had seen him last, with crimson blood staining his yellow robes. Had that really happened only two days ago?

It was on the tip of my tongue to blurt out the truth. I wanted to tell Master Goku everything—about Uncle, and the massacre, and the way Hana and I had run away . . .

But before I could speak, a man in leather armor appeared in the doorway behind Hana. He was dusty from the road, and I guessed that this must be the messenger that Master Goku had sent to our compound last night.

"So sorry to disturb you, Master," the messenger said in a gruff voice. "I have urgent news and thought you would wish to hear it immediately on my return."

My heart began to race. Was he bringing Master Goku news about Uncle, and about Father's death?

Master Goku quickly dismissed Hana and me and drew the messenger into the scroll room.

Just before we left the room, I saw the messenger hand him a crumpled scroll. Hana and I stopped just outside the door to listen.

"I could not deliver the message you sent to the *Jito* yesterday, Master," the messenger said. "The gates to the compound were heavily guarded by samurai who would not let me in. I refused to leave, and noticed that no servants were coming in and out. Something sinister has happened, Master. I am certain of it."

We had to move on because a pair of young masters came down the hall toward us, but we had heard enough. Hana and I stared at each other. Master Goku would know that something was wrong—it was unthinkable for his messenger to be refused an audience with the *Jito*. An insult!

We made our way back toward the kitchens, cutting through the rock garden where gray stones and boulders had been carefully placed on a bed of finely raked gravel.

"Uncle is already insulting his subjects and arousing their suspicions," Hana whispered as we crunched along the pathway. "Why hasn't he revealed his treachery? Why isn't he telling anyone that he is the new *Jito*?"

"I'm certain he won't wait long. He must be gathering strength and consolidating his power," I said. "When he finally makes his announcement, he will want to be sure that no one doubts his authority."

Hana turned to me and touched my hand. "No

matter what, sister, we must keep our heads down and carry on being servant boys."

I nodded.

Choji was waiting for us in the kitchen doorway. "Ah, skinny boys!" he boomed. "You've returned to me at last. Come along. Hurry! Hurry!"

He gestured for us to go past him into the kitchen, where Ko was stirring a huge vat of rice, his face red from the steam. Another servant was on his knees by a low brazier, turning pieces of fish with a long-handled fork.

"It's time to prepare lunch," Choji said.

Hana and I had no more time to think about Uncle and his plans, because laid out on the table ready for us were several enormous piles of vegetables that tottered almost as high as our heads: brown ginger root, white cabbages, pickled green cucumbers, red-brown lotus roots, and giant daikon radishes.

I guessed the vegetables had been placed there for us to peel and chop but Hana and I were both apprehensive—we had never prepared food before. At home, delicious meals had just appeared from the kitchens as if by magic. But, as with the tea and cleaning duties, we would simply have to improvise. Quickly we grabbed a pair of knives from the table and began to work on the cabbages, chopping them into tiny pieces which we tossed into a shallow lacquered dish.

"No, no, skinny boys!" Choji exclaimed when he saw what we were doing. "Not like that! Your heads are so full of Master Goku's teachings that you're ruining my lovely cabbages!" He seized a knife and showed us how to slice. "Like this," he instructed. "Coarse and thick. For texture in the food. If you must shred something, shred the ginger so that the full flavor will come out in the cooking."

Once we were chopping and shredding to his satisfaction, he left us to work alone. Sounds drifted in through a nearby open screen—the quiet strumming of a *koto* harp, students calling encouragement to one another as they sparred in the practice hall, the clash of *bokken* in one of the courtyards. My heart yearned to be out there with them, learning, moving forward on the pathway to becoming a warrior. . . .

I saw Hana looking out of the screen opening. "I wish we could be out there now," I murmured to her, and she nodded.

I wanted to be learning how to send an arrow winging toward a target as accurately as Tatsuya had done. Or practicing our *kata* until we could move with the same grace and deadly speed as our cousin Ken-ichi. We had to hone our skills to protect our family, to avenge our father!

I was so distracted that my vegetable peeling was

clumsy and slow. But the short blades of Choji's vegetable knives were razor sharp and gradually my hands began to move faster.

And suddenly I had an idea. I turned to Hana and grinned.

When I had her attention I flipped my knife up in the air, caught it deftly, and held it like the *tanto* dagger that samurai warriors used for close-quarter fighting. Firmly grasping a long white radish, I slashed swiftly through the fat vegetable, imagining that it was an enemy's exposed throat. Then I pared it into a hundred pieces, my fingers moving so fast they were a blur.

"We *can* train," I whispered to Hana. "Here and now, in the kitchen."

Hana caught on quickly, seizing another radish and holding it out as if it were a sword. I lunged and sliced off the end of the radish, dancing forward to catch the severed end in my fist before it hit the ground. Blade flashing, I whittled the radish all the way up to within a hairsbreadth of Hana's hand, grabbed the remainder, tossed it into the air, and impaled it as it fell.

With a gentle smile, Hana picked up a blade of her own and soon all the radishes lay slaughtered on the table. We practiced the footwork that Father had taught us, shuffling and sliding, turning in half-circles as we moved back and forth between the bowls of vegetables. In the same way, we quartered the pickled cucumbers and made matchsticks from the lotus roots while Ko stared at us in astonishment from the other side of the kitchen.

Choji caught sight of us. He watched for a moment, and then shook his head. "Crazy boys," he tutted, but there was a good-humored sparkle in his eyes. "If you weren't so fast, I'd have to complain to the Master about you. . . ." Then he said, "I'm looking forward to teaching you in my class later."

I glanced at Hana in surprise, and Choji nodded. "Yes, indeed. After the midday meal I take the servants to the small courtyard for their daily weapons training. Master Goku insists that everyone in his school train to the highest standards in the martial arts, including the servants."

Bursting with excitement, Hana and I raced through the rest of the vegetables and hurried to help Ko carry bowls of rice and fish to the eating hall, where the students chattered loudly throughout lunch. We cleared everything away afterward, gulped down our own food, and then scoured the dishes and bowls with sand and vinegar until they shone.

"You need to change into a short-sleeved kimono," Ko told us when we'd finished our work. "And bring your swords!"

Hana and I hurried to our room and changed.

We met up with Ko on the walkway outside and at last all three of us scurried to the small courtyard, along with the nine other household servants. Choji was waiting for us, a row of tall *naginata* spears propped against a rock beside him.

I felt a thrill of excitement at the thought of taking one of those elegant weapons in my hand again. I knew how to handle a *naginata*—

Suddenly I remembered that a poor farmboy would never have even held such a weapon, let alone used one! They were used by foot soldiers and even by horsemen but a shorter version had become a woman's weapon, used to defend her home when her samurai husband was on the battlefield. All the women in my father's household had been well trained in the *naginata*. Hana and I would have to hold back, or we might give ourselves away.

I shot my sister a warning glance and she nodded as if she had been thinking the same thing.

The head servant smiled as we all took our places, kneeling on the ground before him.

"You have probably not trained with one of these before," Choji said, and I tried to feign the same ignorance and curiosity as Ko. "The *naginata* is a versatile weapon, part spear and part cudgel."

He picked up one of the *naginata* and weighed it expertly in one hand before propping it in front of him. Its black wooden shaft and long blade gleamed. "Women in the home will often use it, because they can keep any intruders at arm's length. And not so long ago the *sohei* warrior monks used it to beat, slash, and stab their enemies into submission. There are tales of great battles, where warriors would swing their *naginata* and slay ten or twelve opponents at a time!"

Choji demonstrated different hand grips but then, without warning, he launched into a sudden and breathtaking attack upon an imaginary enemy, swinging the weapon over his left arm and stabbing backward.

Knees bent, brows twisted in a frown, he leaped sideways and turned around as if to meet a second enemy head-on. The long curving blade, which rose from the tip of his *naginata*, sparkled in the afternoon sunshine. He dispatched his foe and sprang around to meet yet another.

The weapon became an extension of his arms, whirling like a waterwheel, slashing at imagined limbs and slicing off invisible heads. When he came to a standstill, his powerful chest was heaving.

"Now it's your turn," he said. "Choose your weapons according to your height. Your *naginata* should be at least an arm's length taller than you are."

I leaped to my feet, Hana at my heels, and we

both hurried to select *naginata*. Choji positioned us so that we were all standing in a row, strung out across the courtyard with a space the length of a *naginata* shaft between each of us. "We don't want any collisions," he explained gruffly. "No severed limbs, please, because there's work to do this afternoon!"

He instructed us in detail about how we should position our hands, the need to stay light on our feet, and how important balance and focus were once a fight was in progress. Hana and I held our *naginata* with deliberate awkwardness, trying to look the part of unskilled peasant boys who knew everything about farm tools and nothing about fancy weapons such as this.

"Today we will learn three basic moves," Choji said, demonstrating a deadly looking sequence as he spoke. "First, the forward step with an upward slash. Second, slide this hand down, take a wide-legged stance, swing the shaft backward beneath your arm, and stab forward with the blade. Finally, slide the right foot forward, angle the toes of the left foot out a little, and swing downward at an angle as if you are harvesting a field of wheat. Now— follow me!"

Stepping in time, we advanced across the courtyard behind Choji. I watched the other servants from the corner of my eye, checking to see how well they handled their weapons. Hana and I copied their mistakes where we could, all the while pretending we were striving for perfection.

I could hear Ko muttering beneath his breath. "Upward slash, swing the shaft, stab, and then swing downward."

"Terrible! Terrible!" roared Choji. "Terrible, all of you. Out of time, out of step, whirling your arms . . ." He shooed us all back to our starting point. "Where's your discipline, eh? Where's your poise? You're like a barrel of monkeys thrown over a cliff."

I saw Hana's hand flash up to cover her mouth, and had to stifle a giggle myself.

"Again!" Choji ordered, and then when we had done it again—worse than the first time by his account—we had to do it another six or seven times. A few of the servants grumbled and Choji made a tutting sound. "You'd better get used to it," he said sternly. "This is the *kenshu* period of intensive training. We train hard . . . and then we start all over again. And the second time around we train *harder*."

"My arms are aching," complained Ko. "I understand about *kenshu*, but can't we go on to another move? Why do we have to do the same thing over and over?"

"You will repeat these three basic moves until you can do them blindfolded," Choji barked. "Your

143

technique must be more than perfect. In real combat your enemy will exploit your slightest weakness, your tiniest hesitation. Do you think an opponent will wait for you to consider your movements? No, he will not. And when he attacks, you won't have time to think about sliding your foot here, or your hand there . . . you must move without thinking, as if in a trance!"

"I will be in a trance by the time we've finished here," Ko grumbled quietly.

But I saw him refocus himself, clenching his jaw, and keeping his head down as he hacked and sliced through the moves, over and over. He was a compact little fighter, younger than Hana and me, but probably three times as tough. I tucked my chin down and refocused too, pretending to improve my technique. Choji noticed and gave me a quick nod of acknowledgment.

By the time the gong rang to signal the end of the afternoon's lessons, my legs ached and my arms were like jelly. Ko and the other servants were red faced, their foreheads damp with sweat. A few wisps of Hana's long black hair had escaped from her topknot and I prayed silently that no one else would see how feminine it made her look.

Choji grinned as he surveyed us. "You're tired," he growled. "And judging by the looks on your faces,

I imagine that you hate me right now." He shrugged and grinned. "You'd hate me even more if I didn't try to get the very best out of you. To be warriors, worthy of your place in Master Goku's school, you must learn to ignore tiredness, pain, the burn in your limbs. I will train you hard, sometimes beyond your endurance, but when you find yourself in combat, you'll thank me for it . . . because every move you make will come as second nature. And you will defeat your enemy."

His words were still ringing in my ears later that evening as we followed Ko along walkways, the moon hanging high in the sky.

"It is customary for the entire school to attend meditation at the end of each day," Ko told Hana and me. "We didn't have it yesterday because of the opening ceremony. Follow me; the meditation room is through here."

We went down a series of wide, shallow wooden steps where small lanterns lit the way along the paths. At last we came to the meditation room. Large and airy, with serene paintings of waterfalls on one of the walls, the place reminded me of my father's working chamber at home. There was the same lingering smell of incense and the same sense of deep peace.

The students kneeled in a large circle around where Master Goku stood, his hands hidden in the sleeves of his black kimono. Beside him, a low lac-quered table was laid ready for tea making with bam-boo ladles and small drinking bowls, and a cast-iron cauldron hung on a hook over a pyramid of smol-dering coals.

The servants sat in a row along one wall, in the *seiza* kneeling position, facing the center of the room, and the three of us joined them silently. Nearby a candle flickered inside a lantern and a moth dipped on fluttering wings.

"Good evening." Master Goku looked around, seeming to take in every face with his calm gaze. "For those of you who have meditated before, you know what is expected of you this evening. For those of you who have not, please allow me to explain. You will sit in silent contemplation, eyes closed, body relaxed as you focus on your breathing and open your mind. Slowly, very slowly, you will allow the con-scious self to slip away, to dissolve, and become free of all thought."

Master Goku began to walk quietly around the room, threading a pathway between the students. "You may begin," he said, his voice low and almost hypnotic, "in your own time. . . ."

There was a general loosening of shoulders among the students. I saw Ken-ichi rest his hands lightly on his knees. Tatsuya's eyes drifted closed. Beside me,

Hana kneeled, the backs of her hands resting on her thighs and her palms open toward the ceiling.

I closed my eyes and took a deep breath, suddenly aware of how exhausted I was. Every bone, muscle, and tendon in my body seemed to ache. I squeezed my hands into fists for a moment and then let them relax, palms upward like Hana's.

"That's right, relax . . . ," Master Goku said. His circuit of the room had brought him close to me. I could hear the silken hem of his long kimono whispering as he passed by. For a moment it was as if everyone else in the room had melted away and he was talking directly to me. "Allow your tired muscles to soften and be still . . . clear your mind of all emotion, all thought, all memories. . . ."

As his voice flowed over me, I tried to let my conscious thoughts slip away. A black veil began to cover my mind, until a glittering blade suddenly slashed an arc across it. With nothing physical to distract me, horrible memories came tumbling one after the other: my father, his face twisted in agony . . . Harumasa bent double, his face ashen with pain . . . Nobuaki being savagely cut down by Uncle.

"Keep breathing," Master Goku's voice interrupted the torrent of blood in my mind. "Very slowly. Inhale. And then exhale. Try counting as you breathe in . . . two, three, four. And breathe out . . .

two, three, four. Think only of the breathing; that is all. Nothing else matters. You are safe here. You may relax, free from the cares of the world."

I did as Master Goku said and slowly I felt my mind dissolving until there was nothing left except the breathing. Inhale . . . two, three, four. Exhale . . . two, three, four. I could no longer feel my aching bones. Memories faded away. Space welled within me and all around me.

Abruptly that space was no longer empty. Something was coming toward me. Blood began to pound in my ears and suddenly all I could think of was the scarred samurai, attacking us at the shrine.

No! my mind screamed, and without thinking I leaped to my feet and yelled wildly as I confronted the intruder, hands hard as steel and positioned ready to fight.

I opened my eyes to see Master Goku standing in front of me—and the astonished faces of all the other students.

CHAPTER TWELVE

Somewhere a boy sniggered and I flushed a deep red, knowing in my heart that it was Ken-ichi.

I covered my embarrassment by bowing deeply to Master Goku. "I am truly sorry," I said. "I don't know what came over me. . . ."

"An apology is not necessary," the Master said. "I am impressed with your sharp reactions. It can take years to teach a student to move so instinctively, without thought. I am pleased to see that skill was born within you."

Relief flooded through me. the Master had managed to turn my humiliation into pride.

Master Goku looked around at the gaping students. "Please return to your meditation," he said quietly, and nodded with satisfaction as they all lowered their heads and closed their eyes once more.

When the meditation session was over, the Master kneeled down carefully at the lacquered table where the tea bowls and ladles had been precisely laid out on a clean white cloth. "As you may know, tea from China is becoming popular among the noble leaders that we, as samurai, must serve. I have spent some time at the temples among the Zen monks and have observed that the process of pouring tea for one's superiors requires control, humility, and precision—just like the martial arts we study. This evening we are going to practice something called *cha no yoriai*, the proper way of pouring tea and showing respect," he said, arranging the folds of his kimono around him. "Every evening of the *kenshu* I will select one student to make and serve tea. The care and precision shown while performing the ceremony will help reveal who among you is the most dexterous fighter and worthy to be called a samurai."

Master Goku gestured for Choji to perform a demonstration.

Ken-ichi made a point of rolling his eyes while Choji explained each step to the gathered students. Our family had been pouring tea in this way for years, and the *cha no yoriai* was not new to my cousin.

"Now," Goku announced when Choji had finished explaining, "one of you shall try to imitate Choji's graceful motions."

I saw Ken-ichi straighten his back. He looked keenly at Master Goku, radiating eagerness to be chosen, but Master Goku called on Tatsuya.

As Tatsuya took his place opposite Master Goku, I could see that he was trying to hide his nervousness, and my heart went out to him. Of course he would have made tea before; who had not stirred and served a bowl of *cha* for their parents? But I doubted whether a boy of his background had ever even seen a *cha no yoriai* before he came to the dojo, let alone taken part. I wished that there was something I could do to help him, but there was nothing to be done. Poor Tatsuya was on his own.

His hands shaking, Tatsuya put a little of the special ceremonial green tea powder into one of the bowls, carefully ladled a scoop of liquid from the boiling cauldron and transferred it into the small bowl. Steam rose in a white curl. I could see from Tatsuya's face that he was struggling to appear calm, to show tranquillity and grace. He whisked the tea in the bowl until it frothed. A whiff of the bitter scent reached my nostrils as he added a ladleful of cold water to make it the right temperature. Then Tatsuya bowed and offered the tea bowl to Master Goku.

Master Goku took the bowl with both hands. He sipped three times, rested, and then sipped three times more. When the bowl was empty he offered it back to Tatsuya, who placed it carefully back on the table. They both bowed, and the ceremony was over.

"You did well, Tatsuya," Master Goku said, after a long pause for consideration. "You understood the steps to pour the tea and you tried to observe the necessary tranquillity, but your inner emotions were plain for me to see. In a true *cha no yoriai*, everything must be perfect for the needs of your guest." He folded his hands into his wide sleeves and narrowed his eyes. "In combat, Tatsuya, would you allow an opponent to see your inner thoughts?"

"No, Sensei," Tatsuya said, shaking his head.

"Of course not," Goku replied. "In all aspects of life, the self must be protected. You can never give an opponent an advantage he hasn't fought for. Do you understand?"

Tatsuya bowed low, clearly disappointed with himself.

I thought Tatsuya had done well, but later, after we had cleaned the hall and helped Ko with the dishes, Hana and I saw a sad-looking figure sitting on the steps that led down to the rock garden. His head was bowed, but there was enough moonlight for us to recognize Tatsuya immediately.

"Are you all right?" Hana asked, and reached out to place a gentle hand on his drooping shoulders.

Instantly Tatsuya straightened his back and tried to look as if he hadn't a care in the world. "Of course," he said brightly, turning to smile up at us. "I'm just admiring the garden before I go to bed." There was a pause, and then his shoulders drooped again. "Actually, no. If you want to know . . . I wish I'd never come here!"

I sat down beside him. Hana sat a few steps below and looked up at Tatsuya, her face full of concern. "You had the privilege of being chosen first," I reminded him.

"And I ruined it," he said in a flat voice. "I was clumsy. I showed my emotions and I spoiled the beauty of the occasion."

"It wasn't that bad," Hana said.

"Everyone in this school has something he needs to improve on." I glanced at Hana. "Silent Fist needs to practice more with the *naginata*. I need to work on my writing. And Ken-ichi needs to improve his manners."

Tatsuya smiled at that. "It just seems that I have so much more to improve on than anyone else here," he said reluctantly. "Sometimes I think I'll never be a samurai."

"You'll learn, and you *will* be a samurai," I told him firmly. "Master Goku wouldn't have selected you for training if he didn't see that in your future."

"Sensei only chose me because of my skills as an archer," Tatsuya said. "He saw me showing off with a bow and arrow one day, hitting targets for money in the marketplace. After his invitation, I begged my mother to let me come here to train. Goku thought I showed potential . . . and maybe I do. Perhaps I *could* be a samurai, if it was just fighting." Tatsuya sighed hopelessly. "But it's not just fighting, is it? There are so many other things that I have to catch up with—learning about tea, reading, and writing. All the other students are from high-ranking families, and it seems as though they were born knowing these things."

"No one is born knowing about those things," I said. "We all have to learn."

"And I want to learn," Tatsuya admitted. "But there's no one to teach me."

"I can teach you," Hana said gently.

Beckoning to Tatsuya, she stood up and made her way down the steps into the rock garden, where a few stone lanterns glowed softly. There, Hana gathered several small rocks and a smooth twig, and placed them neatly on a large flat stone that looked like a low table. She kneeled beside the flat rock and motioned for Tatsuya to take his place opposite.

Silently she showed Tatsuya how to serve tea. She held her sleeve back with one hand and elegantly lifted the twig with the other. She dipped the makeshift ladle close to one of the larger rocks as if it were the cauldron full of boiling water. Her hand was steady, her movements graceful, as she pretended to transfer the liquid into the small stone that represented the tea bowl. I felt a lump in my throat as I remembered past occasions when she had performed *cha no yoriai* for our mother and father at home.

Tatsuya watched carefully, his eyes marveling at Hana's elegant movements. Then Hana indicated that it was his turn. He carefully held back his sleeve and lifted the twig. Hana reached out to place her hands over his, lightly guiding his movements.

"Like this," she said gently.

A few fireflies flickered past, bright against the night sky, and I watched as Tatsuya poured tea with the twigs and stones again and again. Hana seemed to be able to connect with Tatsuya so easily, directing him with little nods and the tiniest touches of her fingers and hands. The sadness had gone entirely from his face, replaced by a determination to get things right.

At last they bowed respectfully to each other. Hana replaced the rocks in the garden, and the teaching session was over.

"Thank you," Tatsuya said with a smile. "I feel as if I have improved a little." He hesitated, and then asked, "How is it that you know so much about the *cha no yoriai?*"

"Well . . . I . . ." Hana floundered, so I broke in.

"It's very important for servants to be able to serve tea properly to important guests," I said.

"And you will become even more skillful if you practice," Hana added, recovering from her confusion.

"Would you help me?" Tatsuya asked.

"Of course," she said. "We can practice together as often as you like."

Tatsuya smiled. "And then next time Master Goku asks me to serve *cha*, I will be ready."

"And when you have leave to go home, you can impress your parents with your knowledge of etiquette," I said.

A shadow of pain flickered across Tatsuya's face. "My mother, maybe," he said. "I don't know about my father. I haven't seen him since I was six years old."

"Oh," I said, and the look of pain on Tatsuya's face brought back a rush of memories of my own father. I swallowed hard. "My brother and I . . . we lost our father recently," I said in a low, hesitant voice.

Tatsuya looked at us both. "I'm sorry," he said gently.

Hana clasped her hands tightly in her lap and looked away across the shadowy garden. I could see that her eyes were bright with tears, but she had a determined look on her face as if she would not let them fall.

"Tell us about your father," I said to Tatsuya.

Tatsuya bit his lip for a moment, as if wondering where to start. Then he took a deep breath. "It's a long story," he said at last. "Let's walk while I tell you."

I nodded, and we all stood up and strolled along a sandy pathway that led through the rock garden. I could hear the light trickle of water somewhere, almost musical in the darkness.

"My father disappeared," Tatsuya told us as we went through an archway and down a series of shallow steps. "One night he told my mother that he was going for a walk. 'At midnight?' she asked him. 'But why?' My father didn't answer. He just took his short sword and an old leather helmet that hung on the wall above the door, and walked out of the house. That was the last my mother saw of him."

"Did he have an accident?" I asked as we crossed a low wooden bridge over a lily pond. Moonlight made the water gleam like silver.

Tatsuya shook his head. "There was never any sign of an accident," he said. "Many moon phases passed, and there was no word from my father. No body was ever found. My mother thought for a long time that he had been set on by robbers, but there's only one road in and out of our tiny village and there was never any sign of a struggle. Nobody heard anything. Nobody saw anything. It was just as if my father had never existed."

"What do you think happened?" Hana asked.

"I saw what happened," Tatsuya said quietly, pausing at the crest of the bridge and looking up at the stars. "I heard him leave, so I kneeled at the doorway and watched him walk along the pathway toward the old Shinto shrine at the edge of the village. I was curious, so I crept out of the house and followed him. He went to the shrine, kneeled for a while in silence, and soon . . . soon another man came. This man was dressed entirely in black, even his face and hands were covered."

We stepped off the wooden bridge and onto a shadowy pathway that led through the gardens.

Tatsuya went on, "I thought he was going to hurt my father, and I was about to shout a warning. But then the man and my father bowed to each other, very formally. The man in black said, 'It is time for you to tread the path toward your destiny, brother,' and my father nodded. Then I accidentally stepped on a dry twig, snapping it in two and both men looked toward the place where I had been hiding . . . and then the strangest thing happened. Something moved behind me, very fast. A hand touched my neck, pressed once, very lightly." Tatsuya reached up briefly to touch the spot, as if he could still feel the hand on his neck even now.

"The next thing I knew," he said, "I was waking up in the dawn light, and my mother was scooping me up into her arms. She was weeping because she thought she'd lost me, when actually, it was my father she had lost."

We had reached the moss garden, where smooth stones and boulders covered with velvety green moss were just visible in the moonlight. The garden was peaceful, the stones carefully grouped so as to harmonize the human spirit with nature. To our left was a sandy courtyard, and beyond that I could just make out the main gate of the dojo, half hidden by a sweeping maple tree.

"Did you ever see your father again?" Hana asked.

Tatsuya shook his head. "Never," he said. "But I don't think he's dead, because every year on the anniversary of the day he disappeared, a bag of coins appears on my mother's pillow during the night. She leaves a candle burning, and sometimes she tries to stay awake to see who enters our house so stealthily—but she never catches them."

"Do you think it's your father?" I asked, fascinated by the story.

"It could be," Tatsuya said. "Or it could be the

man in black who took him away. Who knows?"

He would have said something else, but just then the peace of the night was torn apart by the pounding of horses' hooves. I could hear them approaching fast, at a gallop, and thundering along the road outside the dojo, coming to a sudden halt at the main gate.

"Open up!" yelled a harsh voice, and we heard the sound of hammering on the tall wooden gate. "Open up in the name of the *Jito*!"

Hana grabbed my hand. As we watched, a lantern flared and two guards raced out of a tiny wooden building just inside the gate. One of them was hurriedly buckling on his steel and leather helmet. The other opened the small door set into the gate. There was a low, muttered conversation, and the guard with the helmet raced across the courtyard and disappeared through the wooden archway.

He returned in moments with Master Goku, who had obviously heard the commotion and had met the guard on the way.

"Something's happening," Tatsuya said quietly. "Let's get a bit closer. We might be able to hear what they're saying."

I nodded. "We should stay hidden, though."

We crept nearer, keeping to the shadows of the high wall. I hoped we were camouflaged by the rocks and branches that surrounded us.

More lanterns were lit and Master Goku ordered the gates to be swung open. Immediately a dozen or more mounted samurai streamed into the main courtyard, their hooves churning up the carefully raked sand. My heart began to pound as I recognized the captain with the red silk sash tied around his arm.

These were Uncle's men, the same ones Hana and I had seen terrorizing the village just days ago.

The captain leaped down from his horse and marched across the courtyard to Master Goku. They bowed briefly to each other.

"How can I help you at this late hour?" Master Goku asked, his face tranquil as usual.

"We seek fugitives from the *Jito*'s compound," the captain replied. His voice was harsh and guttural. "Four slaves were convicted of stealing—a woman and her children, including a young boy of six years old. They were imprisoned to await their punishment but escaped and are now on the run."

He was talking about us—and Mother and Moriyasu! Hana's hand tightened on my arm and instinctively we drew back into deeper shadow. Tatsuya was crouching behind a rock, his body so still that he seemed to be at one with his surroundings.

"The *Jito* must have been surprised to hear that

161

women and children had managed to escape from his highly trained soldiers," Master Goku said in a mild voice. "Particularly slaves, who generally have no training in the use of weapons."

The captain looked angry. "Those slaves murdered one of my men," he snapped. "They are dangerous criminals who must be captured at once!"

"And you think these dangerous criminals have come here?"

"It is possible," the captain acknowledged.

"All things are possible," Master Goku said, folding his hands inside his wide sleeves. "But we have seen no wanderers of the sort you describe. No woman has come to my gate, with or without her children."

The captain nodded curtly. "Then they must still be roaming the countryside," he said. "I ask for six of your best students to help with the search."

"Of course," Master Goku said. "The *Jito* knows that my students are his to command." He paused, and then asked, "Has Lord Steward Yoshijiro returned from his trip across the province?"

But the captain didn't hear the question, or pretended not to. He spun around quickly and snapped an order to two of his men, who immediately dismounted.

"Please allow my samurai to help you select the strongest students," the captain said.

Master Goku looked as though he was going to say something else, but instead he bowed his head and turned away to pick up a lantern. As he did so, something caught his attention and he stared out across the courtyard toward our hiding place—

His gaze met mine, and held.

I caught my breath and forced myself to remain motionless. Blood hammered in my ears and I was close to panic. He saw me; he knew! Would he say something to the captain?

Please, I begged the Master silently. *Please don't tell. . . .*

CHAPTER THIRTEEN

I blinked and then the moment passed. Master Goku picked up the lantern without speaking to the captain. He made his way across the courtyard in the direction of the students' quarters, the two samurai falling into step behind him.

Time seemed to move very slowly every second Uncle's samurai were on the school grounds. One word from Goku, and my sister and I were caught.

The captain rapped out orders to his men. Six students came hurrying into the courtyard, fully dressed in kimonos, breeches, and breastplates. Most of them were alert, although one rubbed the sleep from his eyes. Master Goku did not return, and within moments the samurai were turning their horses and galloping out of the gates with the students hurrying after them.

The guards shot the enormous iron bolts back across the gates and doused the lanterns, leaving the courtyard in darkness.

Hana turned to stare at me, her face as pale as the moon. *Uncle is so close to finding us . . .* , her gaze seemed to say. She was about to speak out loud when I shook my head slightly and turned to Tatsuya. He left the cover of the rocks where he'd been crouching and came closer to us.

I knew he sensed our fear, but he didn't say a word. He simply nodded, as if he understood in some way, and then the three of us made our way back through the gardens to our quarters.

Instinctively I knew that Hana and I had made a true friend. One who would never betray us.

The samurai didn't return, but the knowledge that they were still looking for us hung over Hana and me like a waiting sword. I wondered whether Goku would summon us or send guards to seize us. But when nothing happened, I began to think that perhaps the Master hadn't seen me after all.

"I'm sure he saw you," Hana said quietly, when I voiced my anxieties to her as we got dressed the next morning. "But for his own reasons, Goku has chosen not to say anything."

"We should have a plan," I said as I twisted my hair up into a topknot. "If there is ever a raid on the school and we're not together, then we should each try to escape, separately, and make our way to a meeting point. We'll wait there for a day and a

165

night . . . and if the other doesn't come, then the sister that remains must go to the town alone and find Mother."

Hana nodded. "Where should we meet?" she asked.

I thought about that for a moment. "The hill where we stood when we first saw the dojo," I said at last. With this plan in place, we went about our duties, praying that beyond the walls of Master Goku's school, Mother and Moriyasu would continue to evade Uncle and his men.

The moon grew smaller each day and Hana and I were awake every day before dawn, using our duties to exercise and hone our bodies. We washed and chopped vegetables for lunch, attended weapons training with Mister Choji, and practiced meditation.

Occasionally Goku would invite us to a class with the students, and these were the most intense. Under Goku's careful guidance, we trained without weapons, learning basic postures and control over our opponents through precise body positioning. Our muscles grew stronger while our minds became ever more tightly focused.

In the evenings, Hana and I spent time with Tatsuya, who never breathed a word of what he had seen in the courtyard that night. Often we sparred together, exchanging our days' lessons. Sometimes we went to the rock garden to help him practice the *cha no yoriai* and occasionally we would simply sit and talk. Tatsuya told us stories about the world he had come from, and more and more I wished that we could tell him the truth about us.

Tatsuya had a gift as a storyteller, making the most ordinary tales come to life with his vivid descriptions. Once he told us about a plague of frogs that had come to live in the ditches around the paddy fields. They kept everyone in the village awake all night with their croaking.

"I tell you, those frogs could sing," Tatsuya said with a grin. "Someone should have boxed them up, taken them to Heiankyo, and put them on the stage. They'd have kept the Imperial Court amused for many nights!"

Then Tatsuya did an impression of what he thought the frogs might sound like, singing a song to the emperor and his ladies, and performed a little dance.

For the first time since we came to the dojo, Hana laughed. She covered her mouth with her hand and giggled until her eyes watered.

I could have hugged Tatsuya then, for making my sister forget her sadness, just for a while.

One morning, after we had hidden at the dojo for

several days, I woke just as the crimson light of early sunrise began to fill our room. I knew that on our seasonal calendar at home, this day was the first of the period of *Keichitsu*, which means "insects emerging from their holes." I wondered what the day would bring.

Hana was already up. Dressed in her loose blue breeches and jacket, she had put on a pair of *tabi* split-toe socks and was practicing sliding her feet across the floor. This, Tatsuya had told us, was *suri-ashi*, a skill he was learning from one of the young masters. A warrior could use this movement to cover any distance without actually lifting a foot off the floor. In this way, the warrior would remain always rooted to the ground.

I propped my hands behind my head and watched Hana for a while, marveling at her simple, graceful, gliding movements. Her balance was perfect, her feet in constant contact with the ground.

Suddenly she caught sight of me watching her. "Oh!" she said, her cheeks dimpling in a smile. "You're awake! Come on, get out of bed and practice with me."

Grinning, I scrambled out of bed and began to tug my clothes on.

In the red glow of dawn, Hana finished her *suri-ashi* practice and came to help me comb my long hair. "Your memories of that terrible night at home are fading, aren't they?" she asked suddenly.

"How do you know?" I asked in surprise.

"Because, each night, you twist and turn in your sleep a little less, and it has been three nights since you've cried out," she said, sliding the steel comb through my hair.

I turned to face her and saw that her eyes were full of concern.

"Don't worry about me, Hana," I said. "I'm strong."

"And what keeps you going is the thought that one day we'll have our revenge on Uncle," she said softly.

"That," I admitted, "and the hope that we'll be reunited with Mother and Moriyasu." I hesitated as an idea came to me. It was something that had been hovering at the edges of my mind for several days. But now, with Hana, the idea suddenly became something clear and strong. "I think we should try to find them," I said, taking the comb from her. "Choji sometimes goes to the town on a pack horse to collect supplies. We could go with him, take a look around, see if we can find out anything about where they may be hiding."

Outside in the hallway, footsteps came hurrying toward our room. Hana and I exchanged a horrified glance. Someone was coming, and my hair was still down! If they came in, whoever it was would be sure to see that I was a girl. Fingers fumbling in panic, I began to twist my hair up into a boy's topknot. Hana hastily grabbed a long steel pin and reached up to fasten the knot.

We were just in time. The next moment there was a rapid knock and Choji slid the door open.

"Quickly, skinny boys" he barked. "I need everyone in the kitchens this minute! We've just had word that an important visitor is expected here for breakfast and *cha*—and there are a hundred things to do between now and then!"

With that, he raced on down the hallway, rapping his knuckles on every door he passed. Hana and I hastily folded up our sleeping blankets and followed him, our hearts racing.

"What important visitor?" Hana asked in a whisper.

I shook my head, trying to quell my feelings of dread. The first day of *Keichitsu*, a voice whispered in my mind. *The coming of insects* . . . "I don't know," I whispered back to Hana. "Perhaps Uncle has sent someone to the dojo?"

In the kitchens, Ko was already at work, standing at the big wooden table. Piles of vegetables were heaped in front of him and a row of kitchen knives glittered in the early-morning light. Another servant was kneeling in front of the brazier, blowing

170

on the smoldering charcoal to make it flare into life.

Choji handed Hana and me two large buckets. "You're to wash down every stone pathway on the dojo grounds, and make sure not a speck of sand or dust is on the walkways," he told us.

"Who is coming?" I asked, trying to sound casual.

But Choji hurried away, too busy to answer.

When he'd gone, Ko stopped chopping vegetables and leaned across the table toward us. "I heard the new *Jito* is coming," he whispered.

"The new *Jito*?" I repeated faintly.

Ko nodded and pointed to the other servant who was still on his knees trying to coax life into the fire. "Sato was out in the main courtyard when the messenger came," he explained. "He heard them talking . . . Lord Steward Yoshijiro is dead! And now Master Goku must swear allegiance to the new *Jito*, Lord Hidehira!" He shook his head. "Ken-ichi will be completely intolerable once he finds out about his father's new position."

Just then, Choji came bustling back into the kitchen. Ko ducked his head down and returned to his chopping.

I simply stood there, stunned. *Lord Hidehira . . .* even hearing Uncle's name made me feel sick. Beside me, Hana had turned the color of a white lotus flower. All the serenity drained from her face, and

171

I knew that the safety and comfort built up over the past days had been swept away the moment Ko uttered Uncle's name.

I reached out and lightly touched her fingertips with my own. Her gaze locked onto mine, the intensity of her emotions plain to see.

"Come on, skinny boys," Choji said, abruptly breaking into the moment. "Fill the buckets and get started. We don't have time to stand around gaping like idiots!"

As I hurried across the kitchen to slop water into the buckets, my mind burst with questions. Ko had said that Uncle Hidehira was coming here so that Master Goku could swear allegiance. But was there some other reason? Had he somehow guessed that this was where we were hiding?

Clutching the handles of both buckets, I hustled Hana out of the kitchens.

"Uncle's coming here," she whispered, as we made our way toward the first of the stone-paved pathways. "What if he recognizes us . . . ? Oh, Kimi . . . !"

Across the gardens I could see that the wooden walkways were crowded with students standing in quiet groups. Some of them whispered together, and it was clear that the whole school had heard that an important visitor was expected.

"We must keep calm," I told Hana as we cut through the rock garden. "There's no reason for

Uncle to look for us here. Don't forget, his samurai have already been here and found nothing."

Hana nodded. "We'll stay out of his way, and everything will be all right."

"We're *not* going to stay out of his way," I said firmly. Hana's eyes widened in surprise, and she began shaking her head. "This could be our opportunity, Hana. At last we can have revenge on him. We can expose him for what he is and restore the honor of the Yamamoto family!"

"How are we going to do that?" Hana asked as we began pouring water down the pathways and sweeping away any leaves or dirt.

I paused at the top of the steps and glanced left and right along the path to make sure we couldn't be overheard.

"I'm going to wait until the right moment," I said quietly. "And then I'm going to run him through with a dagger, just like he did to Father."

"But you don't have a dagger," Hana pointed out.

"Oh yes, I do," I said.

Hana gasped as I slipped my hand into the folds of my jacket and drew out one of Choji's razor-sharp kitchen knives. I had snatched it from the table when no one was looking.

Its blade glittered wickedly in the bright sunshine.

CHAPTER FOURTEEN

"You wouldn't dare to use it against Uncle. Would you, Kimi?" Hana asked anxiously.

"I would," I replied, my voice bitter. "We have been training so that we would be ready . . . so that we could strike fast, as soon as the moment came. And the moment's almost here, Hana."

Hana nodded. "It must be done. For our father and brothers."

I weighed the dagger in my hand, feeling the smooth wooden handle. Of all Choji's kitchen knives, this was my favorite. The blade had been sharpened so many times that it was thinner and more tapered than all the other knives, but it sliced through the toughest bamboo with ease.

When all the walkways had been cleaned, we hurried to stand with the rest of the servants so that we could watch Uncle's arrival. The main court-yard was lined with students in crisp brown kimonos and formal, wide-legged, black *hakama*. Many were still whispering to one another, full of curiosity about the important visitor.

I spotted Tatsuya standing with one of the young masters. Not far from him, Ken-ichi was laughing and joking with his two friends. The school's enormous gates had been opened wide. Guards stood at attention on either side of the entrance, spears in their hands.

Master Goku stood beneath the wooden archway at the far side of the courtyard, wearing formal robes with his gray hair oiled and dressed. His face was unreadable as he waited in calm silence, his hands hidden in the wide embroidered sleeves of his ceremonial kimono.

Suddenly the sound of a conch-shell trumpet split the air, announcing the approach of the *Jito*. An expectant hush fell over the students gathered in the courtyard. The guards at the gate straightened their backs and gazed straight ahead, the long horns of their steel helmets pointing to the sky.

All at once thirty or more mounted samurai came galloping into the courtyard, swords gleaming and quivers of arrows bristling at their backs. Behind them an ornate black-lacquered palanquin was carried high on the shoulders of four bearers in red silk livery. I recognized the palanquin immediately, with its engravings and gold leaf, white silk curtains rippling in the breeze. It was my father's, and had been used to carry him to every state ceremony and occasion that he had attended as *Jito*.

With pain in my heart, I watched as bearers and palanquin came to a halt in the middle of the courtyard. More samurai soldiers on horseback rode through the gates, swelling the ranks to perhaps sixty or eighty, and I wondered how I was going to get close enough to Uncle to carry out my plan amid so many retainers.

I was still wondering when the curtains of the palanquin were opened and the *Jito* emerged. Surprise rippled through the assembled students, and I guessed that they had been expecting my father, Lord Yoshijiro.

I held my breath and studied my uncle. He was wearing red silk robes and his black hair had been shaved across the brow, oiled into a tail, and folded back on itself on top of his head. Two swords were strapped to his waist.

On the outside, he looked the same as ever . . . but there was something different about him now that he was the *Jito*. He held his head high and proud, without a shadow of guilt for what he had done. As I looked at him, I knew in my heart that when the time came, I would not hesitate to strike.

I would kill him as ruthlessly as he had killed my father and brothers.

Uncle's dark gaze swept the courtyard, probing

the faces of the assembled students and masters. I quickly shrank back behind Ko and Choji, pulling Hana with me.

I couldn't bear to look at Uncle any longer, so I looked at Ken-ichi instead. And I knew by his stunned expression that he had been expecting *my* father to step down from the carriage, not his own. His shock quickly turned to a look of darkness and dread, as if he was afraid of his father. But even that expression passed and in its place came curiosity, and then arrogance. Ken-ichi could see that he was important now—no longer merely the nephew of the *Jito* but the *Jito*'s son!

Uncle Hidehira gazed around the courtyard for a moment longer, his eyes glittering like black ice. Then he spotted Ken-ichi and beckoned him out of the crowd.

Ken-ichi strode across the courtyard to stand before his father. They bowed formally.

"You are my son and heir, Ken-ichi," Uncle said. "Watch me. Learn from me. And one day you will also stand here as *Jito* and accept the allegiance of the samurai students."

Some of the students struggled to mask their disgust; others glanced at Ken-ichi with new respect.

"Thank you, Father," Ken-ichi said, bowing again. As he returned to his friends, he looked even more smug and superior than before.

Not for long, cousin, I thought. *Soon your father will be exposed as a murderer, and we'll see how superior you look then.*

Master Goku walked forward, his robes flowing behind him. He came to a halt five paces from Uncle and bowed deeply. "I welcome you to the dojo, Yamamoto no Hidehira, Lord Steward to the Shogun," he said, his voice calm and measured. "I offer my own loyalty, and that of my students and servants. And I offer my sword. . . ."

Kneeling, the Master laid his long *nihonto* sword at Uncle's feet. He placed his hands flat on the ground and leaned forward until his forehead touched the ground, just in front of the ornate scabbard.

Uncle watched, looking pleased. He bowed, and then gestured for Master Goku to rise. "Thank you, Master," he said in his deep, powerful voice. "I accept your allegiance, and I know that when the time comes you will wield your sword wisely on behalf of the house of Yamamoto."

Master Goku replaced his sword in his belt, stood up, and as he bowed again, he brought his index fingers slightly together flat against his thighs as a sign of respect. "When the time comes," he echoed. But his voice was strangely flat and I sensed a resistance in him, as if he privately hoped the time would never come when he had to fight on Uncle's behalf.

The formalities over, Master Goku dismissed the students and masters, telling them that they should practice hard at their chosen skill because the *Jito* would tour the school later that morning. He and Uncle then made their way across the courtyard at a leisurely pace, heading through the wooden archway toward the moss garden.

Most of the samurai stayed behind, but at a signal from Uncle two of them dismounted, tossed their reins to a foot soldier, and followed the Master and the *Jito* at a respectful distance.

Choji turned to us. "Skinny boys, come with me to the tea pavilion," he said. "I will need help serving."

I exchanged an anxious glance with Hana. Surely Uncle would recognize us at such close quarters? We would just have to be invisible, moving like *kami* spirits around a room, and hope that the new *Jito* would not even glance us.

We could not afford to draw attention to ourselves before I had the chance to take my revenge.

We followed the small group of men through the moss garden to the tea pavilion. The morning sun had risen above the trees and there were dappled shadows on the white pebble pathway. Master Goku and Uncle paused to slip off their sandals before

179

climbing the four wooden steps that led up to the tea pavilion and went inside. The two samurai positioned themselves on either side of the steps, hands on the hilts of their swords, and narrow eyes fixed straight ahead.

Following Choji, I moved cautiously between the two soldiers and entered the pavilion with Hana at my side.

Although the doors were left open behind us, the screens were all closed and I blinked once or twice to accustom my eyes to the shadowy interior.

The room was richly carpeted with fresh green tatami mats, ten in all, to precisely fit the dimensions of the room. A tall vase stood in one corner containing a camellia flower, which filled the air with its delicate scent. Two cushions had been placed on either side of a low gold-lacquered table that had been laid with bowls and ladles for the *cha no yoriai*. A cauldron was poised on its hook above a charcoal brazier.

Master Goku and Uncle went to kneel on the two cushions, tucking their heels neatly under themselves. Uncle stared across the table at the Master, radiating power and authority. Master Goku returned his gaze without blinking.

There was a moment of tension; then the Master inclined his head in a half bow and turned to Choji.

"*Cha*, please, Mr. Choji," he said calmly.

"Yes, Sensei." Choji turned to Hana. "Hurry to the kitchens and ask Ko to prepare a dish of rice and bean curd," he said in a low voice.

"Yes, Choji," Hana said respectfully, making her voice sound even deeper and more boyish than usual. She bowed and turned to go, her eyes meeting mine for an intense moment before she headed toward the door. I knew she was offering me her silent support.

When she had gone, the head servant turned to me. "Stand behind the *Jito*," he said. "If he needs anything, you will fetch it."

I bobbed my head and moved smoothly to take up my place. I was so close to Uncle that I could smell the oil he had used on his hair. I watched as he reached into his wide sleeve and drew out a small bamboo fan. He unfolded it and began to fan himself slowly, his gaze still fixed on Master Goku.

"I trust that you are well, Master?" he asked.

"Very well, thank you," Master Goku replied.

"No plans to retire? To live out your twilight years in a comfortable pavilion overlooking the eastern seas?"

"No such plans," Master Goku said mildly. "My place is here at the dojo, and always will be."

"That is good to hear."

There was a pause as they watched Choji kneel and serve tea with grace and expertise. I watched Uncle as he leaned forward to accept his bowl from Choji's steady hands. I studied the way his robes shifted as he moved. I focused on his back, just beneath his rib cage, where my blade could be plunged through the red silk into the soft flesh beneath. I held that target in my mind.

"I have great plans to expand my power," Uncle said to Master Goku, as Choji withdrew. "And to do that, I shall need your help. I want an army of skilled samurai to fight for me—samurai trained in your school, Master. I have decided that you will take on another fifty students. You may begin your search for the best candidates immediately."

For a moment I thought Master Goku was going to choke on his tea. "Fifty students?" he said in astonishment. "But the school is already full. I don't have room for any more students!"

"You'll make room," Uncle said crisply. He lifted his tea bowl and took a sip of *cha*. "Build more practice halls . . . extend the courtyards . . . employ more servants and teachers. It's really quite simple."

"Simple, perhaps. But why such a hurry, Lord Hidehira?" Master Goku asked. "Expanding the territory will mean war, seizing estates from other *Jito*—"

"I don't see a problem with that," Uncle interrupted, looking annoyed.

Master Goku was incredulous. "But—"

"Enough!" Uncle snapped. "You forget your place, Master Goku. I will not be questioned by one of my subjects."

The Master looked shocked but recovered quickly. "Your brother, Lord Yoshijiro, would never have—"

"My brother is dead." Uncle's voice was harsh and loud. "Whatever he may or may not have done is in the past. The lands and title belong to me now and will be ruled with a firm hand from this day onward. Yoshijiro was too soft, too slow, always tiptoeing about the other *Jito* and the courts, being polite. I have no such intentions."

Rage simmered inside me as I listened to him.

"I was sorry to hear of your brother's passing," Master Goku said calmly. "He was a wise man."

"He was a fool," Uncle said with a sneer. "Koishi. Little Stone. How I despised him . . ."

"And what of your nephews, Harumasa and Nobuaki?" Master Goku asked. "Will they be coming back to train at the dojo?"

Uncle leaned forward. "They died with their father," Uncle said. "There is no one left with a claim to the title of *Jito*, and if you ever question my authority again, old man, I will kill you myself."

My heart ached to see how completely Uncle's disguise had slipped. There was no more mask of pretense—now I could see how hateful and evil he truly was.

I could contain myself no more. I checked the two samurai stationed outside the door, but they were out of sight. Quickly I reached inside my jacket and put my hand around the smooth wooden hilt of the knife.

The moment had come.

I would have my revenge!

CHAPTER FIFTEEN

I was up on the balls of my feet, ready to launch myself forward when Master Goku's tranquil voice broke into my fury. "Kagenashi."

I reacted the instant he uttered my adopted name. My gaze met his, and I saw that his eyes were hard, like jade.

"Go to the kitchen and fetch some food for our distinguished guest," he said sharply.

I hesitated, my hand still firm on the hilt of the knife.

Could I let this moment pass?

Kill him now, a silent voice inside my head urged. *Kill Hidehira! Before he sees your face and realizes who you are. You may not have another chance.*

Master Goku repeated my name, "Kagenashi . . ." and Uncle, suddenly aware of an undercurrent of tension in the room, stopped fanning himself. He half turned to look at me, and I felt my grip on the dagger tighten.

Then a calm voice gently pushed its way to the

forefront of my mind. *To kill him here, in the presence of Master Goku, would bring great dishonor on the dojo.* I hesitated, but then left my knife where it was and withdrew my hand.

I glanced at Master Goku. He nodded, his face unreadable.

At that moment Lord Hidehira turned around to look at me.

Quickly I bowed low to hide my face. Had Uncle recognized me?

Heart racing, I waited for an agonizing moment and at last Uncle turned away and began to fan himself lazily. "Rice and bean curd would be suitable after my journey."

"Go to the kitchens immediately," Master Goku told me. "Send Ko back here in your place."

Keeping my head bowed, I slowly backed out of the tea pavilion. Bitter frustration washed over me, but also a sense of shame. I had been so close to bringing dishonor to the dojo—and somehow Master Goku had known.

The samurai guards did not even look at me as I raced down the steps and pelted along the pathway toward the kitchens. I almost ran full tilt into Hana, who was carrying a big square tray loaded with tiny bowls—white rice, creamy bean curd, and a delicate glass bottle of soy sauce.

"Kimi!" she cried. "Did you do it?"

"I couldn't!" I bent forward and put my hands on my knees as failure and shame rushed over me.

Hana's eyes widened. "What happened?" she asked. Hana quickly put her tray down on a nearby rock and put her arms around me.

"I couldn't do it . . . I couldn't do it . . . ," I blurted. "Goku looked at me . . . and he . . . he . . . !"

Hana took my elbows, making me stand up straight. "He knew, didn't he?" she said quietly.

I nodded, barely able to breathe. "The knife was in my hand, Hana. I was so close! Uncle was just there in front of me. I was behind him; I knew the perfect place to strike . . . but the Master called my name and looked into my eyes. He knew what I was going to do—and all at once I couldn't do it! All I could think about was the dishonor I would bring down on the dojo." I clung desperately to Hana as another thought occurred to me. "What if Master Goku tells Uncle that one of the servants tried to kill him? I'll be dragged out into the courtyard and Uncle will execute me with his sword."

"No!" Hana cried.

"You know it's true," I insisted. I took a deep breath, feeling suddenly calmer. "Hana, listen to me. If Uncle has me killed, will you promise to get revenge? Not for me—but for our father and brothers. And promise to keep Mother and Moriyasu safe."

"I promise," Hana said firmly. "You know I won't rest until Uncle can never hurt us again. But Kimi . . . I don't think that Master Goku will say anything."

Despite her reassuring words, my stomach was tight with dread at the thought of Master Goku telling Uncle what he had seen. But the rest of the day passed without incident, and I guessed that the Master had kept his silence. Uncle toured the dojo, inspecting the skills of the students with Ken-ichi at his side. Later, when Uncle had climbed into the palanquin and left the dojo, Ken-ichi carried on as if he himself was the *Jito* in his father's absence.

That night he strode around the courtyards and practice halls with his two friends flanking him like bodyguards. He told anyone who would listen that he was heir to the *Jito*, and that one day they would serve him in his samurai army.

"How does that sound? Eh, Tatsuya?" Ken-ichi asked, interrupting Tatsuya, who was practicing the movements of the *kata* in the main practice hall. "You'll swear allegiance to me, won't you?"

Tatsuya bowed. "I will be yours to command," he said, his voice wary, "if I stay in these lands. However, when I am trained, I may decide to travel across the kingdom of Japan to serve elsewhere."

Ken-ichi's face twisted angrily. "You won't find

a worthier lord than a Yamamoto," he snapped. "My father is the most skilled samurai in the world. He killed Lord Yoshijiro battling one-on-one! He told me all about it."

Hana and I were across the hall, busily reaching up to light the lanterns that swung from their tall iron stands, but I stopped to listen when I heard Ken-ichi mention a battle. What battle? There had been no battle. Only dishonor and murder . . .

"The old *Jito* invited my father to a *kaiseki ryori*," Ken-ichi told Tatsuya. "But that most friendly of celebrations turned into an ambush. Lord Yoshijiro had gone mad, like a rabid dog! He attacked my father for no reason, forced him to defend himself."

I stared across the hall at Ken-ichi, rage boiling up inside me. *Lies!* I wanted to shout.

"And when my father bested him and offered him the chance to die an honorable death, to commit *seppuku* by slicing himself across the belly and going to his death cleansed by pain—Lord Yoshijiro refused!" Ken-ichi let out a snort of disgust.

Hana put her hand on my arm to hold me back.

Across the hall, Tatsuya had an expression of curiosity on his face. "What happened to the rest of Lord Yoshijiro's family?" he asked Ken-ichi.

"Dead," Ken-ichi said briskly.

"All of them?" Tatsuya was astounded.

189

"Every woman and child, and all the servants too," Ken-ichi told him. "The whole household was put to the sword for their part in Lord Yoshijiro's treachery, as is the noble custom."

Tatsuya looked shocked. "The nobles have strange customs."

Ken-ichi shrugged. He turned on his heel and strutted away from Tatsuya, looking like a peacock as he swept through the practice hall. Students scurried out of his way, some of them bowing low as he passed.

It was all I could do not to leap across the hall and attack him, fingers clawing and hands chopping like knife blades.

I had a sudden vision of my foot connecting with Ken-ichi's jaw, all the power of my body surging through my leg as I kicked hard and knocked against his teeth. Bright crimson blood would splatter the polished wooden floor of the practice hall. . . .

A stern voice broke into my thoughts, and I turned to see Master Goku standing in front of me.

"Kagenashi and Otonashi," he said. "Follow me to the meditation room."

He strode away. Hana and I exchanged a quick, worried glance and then followed him. My mind was in turmoil. Had Goku guessed that I wanted to attack the *Jito*'s son? Or, worse, was he going to tell me that he had no choice but to inform Uncle that I had reached for a knife in the tea pavilion earlier? Was he going to throw us out of the dojo?

My hands were trembling by the time we reached the meditation room. I hid them by tucking them into my sleeves. Master Goku turned to look at me.

"Light the lanterns and set the sticks of incense to smolder," he said flatly. "We will meditate."

I bowed, trying to keep my fear under control. After we had done as he asked, Master Goku indicated that Hana and I should sit down, side by side in the center of the room. He took his place opposite, arranged his black robes around him, and was silent for a moment. His eyes were closed, his breathing slow and regular. Hana and I placed our hands on our knees, palms upward, and let our eyelids flutter closed.

The peaceful atmosphere and the sweet perfume of the incense was a balm. I could feel Hana relaxing beside me, her soul soothed, but I was jumpy and could not settle. I tried counting my breaths, as the Master had taught us, but calmness escaped me. Instead my spirit burned.

Why were we here? Was Master Goku keeping Hana and me under his watchful gaze while guards rode hard to the *Jito* to alert him of our treachery?

"Calm yourself, Kagenashi," Goku said, and I

finally settled into relaxed meditation.

I don't know how long we sat in silence, but when I next opened my eyes the long incense stick had burned away to nothing, a line of gray-brown ash lying in its place. It must have been near midnight, and I had the feeling that we three were the only ones awake in a world that slept.

Master Goku was looking at me. I forced myself to meet his gaze, resigned now that he would turn me in because of his loyalty to the *Jito*.

After a moment, his gaze settled on Hana.

They seemed to talk silently, their eyes communicating without a word being uttered. Occasionally Master Goku nodded, and after a while I could see tears welling up in Hana's eyes. Her breathing deepened. Then a single tear overflowed and rolled down her cheek, leaving a sparkling trail on her skin. Her resolve had broken finally, and my sister wept.

Master Goku leaned forward and took her hand in his. "You are safe now, my child," he said gently. "No one will harm you here. You are hidden, and you may remain here in secret for as long as you need."

Still holding Hana's hand, he turned to me and bowed his head respectfully. "As Lord Yoshijiro's daughters, you have my allegiance," he said softly.

"I swear that my sword will defend you, my house will shelter you, and my food will nourish you."

I stared at him, numb with shock and relief. "You know who we are?" I asked breathlessly, my heart beating faster.

"I suspected," he confirmed. "I knew that something strange was happening that day you presented yourself at my gates. But I wasn't sure who you were then. I believed that you were boys . . . but I knew there was something different about you both. I have observed you, and I've been impressed by your humility as well as by your skills."

"But . . . but *how* do you know?" I couldn't think of when we would have given ourselves away so plainly.

"I saw you in the shadows the night that the samurai soldiers came. It was not difficult to make the connection between the so-called servants they were looking for." He smiled gently. "No ordinary six-year-old would be of concern to the *Jito*'s guards. That, added to the incident when my messenger was refused an audience, confirmed my suspicions. I guessed that there had been a power struggle and that Lord Yoshijiro's family had escaped. The boy they were seeking must have been the youngest heir."

I nodded. the Master missed nothing. "I am Yamamoto no Kimi," I said, bowing low to the floor.

"And this is my sister, Hana. We are the daughters of Lord Yoshijiro."

"Kimi and Hana, your secret is safe with me." Master Goku paused for a moment. "I am going to ask something of you now, but it may be painful for you . . . will you tell me the truth of what happened the night your father died?"

My stomach tightened, but I nodded firmly. "You have been so good to us and we are grateful. I will tell you."

My voice seemed strange to me as I talked, quiet and calm despite the rage inside me. I told him everything. "But now that you know who we are, surely you cannot continue to give us shelter," I said. "After all, it is against the *bushi*, the warrior's code, for a samurai to harbor the enemy of his master."

Master Goku shook his head. "I will not turn you out," he said. "For two reasons. First—if it is true that your brother Moriyasu lives, then Lord Hidehira is not the real *Jito*, for the title would pass to the son until he was defeated. Therefore Hidehira is not my master. And second—when he killed your father, Hidehira himself broke the *bushi* code. I owe no loyalty to a murderer."

Relief washed over me. We would not have to run again.

"Thank you, Master Goku," Hana and I said

194

quietly, bowing low and long, with our index fingers touching at the tips to show the greatest respect.

Hana sat up, wiped her tears with the cuff of her jacket, and smoothed back a few wisps of silky black hair that had escaped from her topknot. "Why would Uncle do this to our family?" she asked softly.

Master Goku sighed. "I remember Hidehira and Yoshijiro when they attended this school," he said. "When they were young, they were inseparable. You never saw one without the other. But as they grew older it became clear that Yoshijiro was more skilled in his fighting and more dedicated to his studies. Yoshijiro won the tournament three years in a row, defeating his elder brother in the final bout each time. His father—your grandfather—heaped praises upon him, and over time Hidehira grew jealous. He felt his father favored the younger son unfairly."

Across the room a lantern flickered, making shadows dance upon the walls.

"When your grandfather named Yoshijiro as his successor," Master Goku went on, "Hidehira must have been bitterly wounded. I spoke to him about it, here in this very room. But he masked his anger and his hurt, convincing me that he would support Yoshijiro." Goku frowned, watching the dancing shadows on the walls as if they were the shadows of the past. "That day, I praised his dignity and humility. But now, I must wonder if he was planning his terrible revenge even then."

We were all silent for a while, each of us held captive by our own thoughts and memories of Hidehira.

"What do you intend to do now?" Master Goku asked eventually.

"We want to find Mother and Moriyasu," I said, and told him about the message we had found at the old shrine in the forest. "We think they may have gone to the town. It would be easy for them to hide there."

Master Goku considered this for a moment. "It is easy to hide two people," he said. "But not four. For your own safety, as well as that of your mother and brother, I would urge you to stay here under my protection for as long as possible. And maybe one day you will be able to set things right."

The lantern flickered again and Hana reached out and took my hand.

"But I am not talking about murder, Kimi," Master Goku went on, fixing me with a stern look. "There is no room in the *bushi* code for murder. To attack Lord Hidehira from behind, with a hidden blade, would be dishonorable and cowardly. Such an act would make you as treacherous as he is."

"But my uncle deserves to die for what he did!" I protested.

"Perhaps he does," Master Goku said mildly. "But you will not murder him with a knife in the back at a *cha no yoriai*. And you will not attack his son with feet and fists."

I felt the shame of what I had wanted to do and vowed that I would never allow myself to walk the path of treachery and dishonor.

"No," the Master went on, "if you wish to restore your family's honor, you must challenge Lord Hidehira openly. You must fight him fairly."

I took a deep breath. "You're right, Sensei. I will face my uncle in open combat, and win. If he defeats me, so be it."

"Harness your talents, concentrate your mind, focus on training." Master Goku turned to Hana. "Although it is not yours, the name Silent Fist was truly inspired. Your opponent rarely knows when or where your fist will come from, Hana. You must perfect that skill." His eyes crinkled at the corners as he smiled.

"And you, Shadowless Feet," he said, turning to me. "Your heels ache to kick out, so I think I will set you a target. Tomorrow, when you have finished your chores and Mister Choji releases you, go to the small courtyard beyond the rock garden. In the center,

197

there is a dead but firmly rooted willow tree."

"I've seen it," I said, wondering why he was bringing it up.

"I would like to see you knock down that tree with a single kick," he said. "Your uncle is one of the mightiest warriors in Japan. When he was a student here, long ago, the only man to defeat him in practice sessions was your father. . . . Understand that Hidehira will not be defeated easily. But you are your father's daughter, Kimi. With experience and training, you could be a great fighter. Kick down the willow tree, and you will move closer to your goal of matching Hidehira in combat."

I nodded, determined to seek out the tree in the morning, as soon as I had finished my chores.

"You will both train hard," Master Goku said. "And meanwhile, I will do all I can to help you find your mother and young Moriyasu. I will send letters to various friends in the town, and see what I can discover."

The Master ushered us out of the meditation room and into the cool night air. Hana and I quietly made our way through the gardens and along the walkways. When we reached the servants' quarters, I paused for a moment on the steps and glanced up at the night sky. Stars were sprinkled across the deep blue, like silver fish sewn across a dark kimono. I felt as though a great weight had been lifted from my shoulders.

I let Hana go indoors ahead of me, saying I wanted to stay outside for a moment longer.

When I was alone, I took a deep breath and brought my hands together, bowing my head as I offered up a silent prayer of thanks for Master Goku's support.

CHAPTER SIXTEEN

For Hana and me, life seemed a little easier after our meditation session with Master Goku. Our hearts were filled with hope.

the Master never mentioned our true identities again, and nor did he seem to treat us any differently than he had before. But whenever he looked at us, I could feel his silent approval of the mission we had set for ourselves—and I remembered that he had promised to try to find our mother.

Every evening Hana and I met Tatsuya in the rock garden, or down by the lily pond, sparring with *bokken* and *jo* as well as hand-to-hand combat, knife techniques, and wrestling. Often he brought a straw target and some bows, and Hana and I loosed arrows until long after the other students had gone to bed.

Once, as I was practicing my *bokken kata*, Hana was practicing her Silent Fist techniques. Her feet were silent on the grass, her fists seeking the weak points of an invisible enemy.

A moment later I heard the sound of her running feet. I looked up just as Hana launched herself into the air and scaled the wall like a shadow warrior, using the air as a staircase until she was running along the top. She reached the corner and then flipped herself backward off the wall to land on her feet in the middle of the pathway as lightly as a cat.

I grinned. "Show-off," I said. But seeing my sister run with such skill made me think about the task Goku had set for me.

I remembered how my father had once said to me, "A good warrior knows his enemy, Kimi. He studies him until he knows exactly how he works, what makes him who he is. Only when you truly know your enemy can you ever hope to defeat him!"

With Father's voice ringing through my mind, I went to the dead willow tree and sat for a long time studying it. The tree was not an enemy, but it was a target and so I observed its shape, how it had grown twisted at certain points, where it might be weak, and where it was strong.

I did not feel that I was ready to try to kick it down yet. So instead I begged a few empty caskets from Choji and half filled them with sand so that I could practice on them. At first, the dull thud of falling caskets drew a few students, curious to see who was making the noise. But soon they got used to me and drifted away, back to their own training sessions.

As each night surrendered to a new dawn, I could feel myself becoming stronger, my muscles more toned, my punches and kicks more powerful.

But all the while, our cousin Ken-ichi grew more arrogant and unbearable. He demanded that the other students address him as Ken-ichi-*dono*, adding the term of respect for nobles, and insisted that they make way for him when he was walking along walkways and through narrow halls.

"I take precedence," he would say, "because I am the *Jito*'s son!"

I avoided him as much as possible, because I couldn't trust myself not to disobey Master Goku and attack my cousin with fists and feet!

One day, Choji assigned Hana and me to a new duty instead of cleaning rooms.

"It's a fine spring day!" he declared. "The sun is shining and there's a light breeze. I thought you'd enjoy being outside. . . ." For a moment I thought Choji was going to give us a day off, but then he continued, "It's a perfect day for doing laundry . . . come with me!"

He took us up a winding gravel pathway that led behind the bathhouse and showed us the well for drawing water, the deep wooden barrels where linen was scrubbed with bran bags, and the long, thin drying ropes strung from tree to tree.

"Be finished by midday," Choji said. "And then come to the kitchens to help prepare lunch."

When he had gone, I made a face at Hana. "Bran bags? What about soapwort?"

"I think it's too expensive," she said, rolling up her sleeves and reaching for a bucket. "And bran bags probably work just as well. At least we can have some fun with this. Beating the dirt out of the breeches and bedsheets will strengthen our arms and make us better fighters!"

We worked hard for the rest of the morning, scrubbing and rinsing and hanging the laundry from the trees. It was a struggle to get things right at first, but we quickly realized that kimonos and *hakama* trousers needed to be stretched when they were hung out, so that they would be smooth when the sun had dried them.

Working together, we finished with time to spare, and I challenged Hana to a duel, wielding my long-handled washing paddle as if it was a *jo*. She grinned and grabbed the pair of wooden tongs she'd been using to transfer wet clothes from one tub to another, to use as a *bokken*. We danced back and forth among puddles that sparkled in the spring sunshine, leaped up onto a low wall, and then ducked down beneath

203

the kimonos and table linens.

We stopped abruptly when we heard the sound of three pairs of feet crunching up the gravel pathway toward us.

"Come on . . . follow me!" someone said. We couldn't see the speaker because of the laundry strung from the trees, but the drawling arrogant voice had become as familiar to me as my own.

Ken-ichi.

And it sounded as if he had his two friends with him as usual.

I exchanged a glance with Hana. Quietly we laid down our weapons and retreated behind an extra barrier of hanging laundry. After a moment there came the sound of liquid being poured and the clink of bowls. Someone made a slurping sound and almost immediately began coughing.

"By the Buddha, that's disgusting!" The boy's voice sounded half choked. "How do you know it's sake rice wine, Ken-ichi-*dono*? For all we know, it could be poison."

"Of course it's not poison, you idiot," Ken-ichi said with a snort. "I *can* tell the difference between poison and sake, you know!"

Hana and I exchanged a glance. Ken-ichi and his friends were drinking alcohol!

"How do you tell the difference?" one of the boys

asked. "I thought that was the whole point with poisons. They're easily hidden, and easily mistaken for something else. What if this is . . . poisoned sake?"

I heard Ken-ichi slurp from the bowl. "It isn't," he said stoutly. "I got it from the kitchens. They're hardly going to give the Master something that's poisoned, are they?" He gave a snort. "Although . . . if I *was* going to poison someone, slipping it into a drink like sake would be so easy!"

"You're so clever, Ken-ichi-*dono*," the other boy said in a fawning voice. "You know everything."

"I make it my business to know everything," Ken-ichi said. There was a pause, and then he added, "And right now I know that we're being spied upon!"

Before Hana and I could find another place to hide, he was striding through the hanging laundry, tearing it down from the thin ropes until he was standing face to face with us, three white sheets and a kimono twisted around his arm.

I shoved Hana behind me, snatched up my wooden paddle, and held it in front of me defensively.

Ken-ichi took one look at me and snorted with laughter. "What are you going to do?" he asked. "Lather me with rice bran and paddle me to death?"

"How did you know we were here?" I countered.

"I heard you crashing around before we even got here," he sneered. "You were pathetic! I've seen girls fight better than you two!"

I flushed and forced myself to stare at the ground. It was clear that he was just trying to insult us, but it made my heart jump to think that he might be close to uncovering our secret. Behind him, his two friends sniggered.

Pleased with himself, Ken-ichi went on, "I wonder what that old fool Choji would say if he knew two of his slaves were messing about up here instead of working. Eh?"

I clenched my fist so tightly around the wooden paddle that my knuckles turned white. "We're not slaves."

Ken-ichi looked us up and down. "You look like slaves to me," he said, and glanced at his friends. "What do you think? Do they look like slaves to you?"

"Definitely slaves," one of the boys said with relish. "I think you'd better inspect their work, Ken-ichi-*dono*."

Ken-ichi grinned. "What a good idea," he said, and deliberately dropped the armful of clean laundry he'd been holding. Still grinning, he placed his sandaled foot squarely in the middle of the pile and ground the fabric into a muddy puddle. "Oh dear," he said slowly, his dark eyes spiteful. "I think you *slaves* will have to clean these again!"

Turning on his heel, Ken-ichi walked away. His two friends went scurrying after him, sniggering and nudging each other.

At that moment, I felt like I couldn't contain myself any longer. My fists clenched around my wooden paddle and I thought about smashing it down on his head—but then I stopped. I remembered my vow to myself. I would not dogfight with Ken-ichi. My time for revenge would come.

I felt Hana's hand on my arm. "Leave him," Hana said. She was watching him too, her eyes narrowed thoughtfully. "There is a time and place to see justice done."

"I know," I said. "But he *wants* me to challenge him."

"If that's the case, then you will punish him more by not giving him what he wants," Hana reasoned.

Hana was right. I watched Ken-ichi strut down the pathway and finally disappear around the corner of the bathhouse.

I knew that if I was patient, the opportunity would come to deal with him calmly and effectively. Once and forever.

CHAPTER SEVENTEEN

"You're late," grumbled Choji when we finally appeared in the kitchens to help prepare lunch. "What were you doing up there—washing everything twice over?"

As a punishment, he made us skip our afternoon weapons training and told us to scrub the kitchen floor with hot water and sand. "When I return, I don't want to see a single spot of grease anywhere!"

He turned on his heel and left the kitchen. Hana and I glanced at each other in surprise.

"What's wrong with Choji?" I asked Ko, who was busy kneading noodle dough at the table.

Ko made a face. "He's been like that ever since he came back from the village without any supplies," he said. "One of the other servants said that there's little food available to buy. The village is almost deserted. The *Jito* has samurai soldiers posted on every street corner. They take a percentage of any food that comes in for the *Jito* and what

208

is left over is not enough. . . . People are beginning to go hungry."

We served a small lunch to the students, and all the servants sat in thoughtful silence to eat their own thin fish soup. Choji wasn't present. Ko said the head servant had gone to talk to Master Goku. He was hoping the Master would appeal to Lord Hidehira for more food.

Hana and I worked hard, and by the time we made our way to the meditation room that evening, we were almost dead on our feet. Our arms ached from wringing laundry and our hands were raw from spending most of the day being plunged into buckets of hot water. Our bellies growled with hunger.

As soon as meditation began, I closed my eyes and felt myself drifting away. . . .

After the session, the relaxed atmosphere remained. Students talked quietly as they left the meditation room in small groups. Hana and I went around with the other servants, sweeping up the ash beneath incense sticks and putting out lanterns.

Suddenly Hana dug her sharp elbow into my ribs. A messenger was standing in the doorway, his clothes dusty from the road. He bowed low and approached Master Goku.

"Greetings, Sensei," he said breathlessly. "I bring

word from your friend Master Jin of Sagami to the south."

Master Goku signaled to one of the other servants to bring *cha*. "What does my good friend Master Jin say?"

The man bowed again. "He apologizes, but he cannot continue his correspondence with you. Alliances between neighboring estates are being dissolved upon the word of your *Jito*. Lord Hidehira has announced his intention to seize the surrounding territories for himself. Therefore Master Jin says that he regrets to tell you that from this day onward, you and he must be considered enemies."

Master Goku closed his eyes briefly, and for a moment he looked like an old man. "The alliances are being dissolved." His voice sounded heavy and tired. "And it is as I feared. . . ."

I knew Father had worked hard to build alliances throughout the kingdom, to bring peace to neighboring estates and form relationships with other provinces. But Uncle was destroying everything.

When the servant returned with *cha*, Master Goku dismissed us all and drew the messenger into a quiet corner, obviously to question him further.

Outside in the hallway, Ken-ichi was strutting like a peacock. "Soon the whole kingdom of Japan will be in my father's grasp," he bragged. "Before long he'll be *Jito* of all the estates between here and the southern islands. He'll be Shogun!"

Behind me, Ko and another servant boy, Sato, were whispering.

"Lord Hidehira has raised taxes on all farmers," Sato said. "My father is headman of our village and he says the new taxes will cripple them!"

"I heard that the local people have a new name for the *Jito*," Ko said with a nod. "They are calling him Kaminari."

Kaminari . . . Thunder. It seemed an appropriate name for Uncle. He was unleashing a storm upon our lands.

Up ahead, Ken-ichi suddenly wheeled around, his dark eyes flashing. "Who said that?" he demanded.

Ko turned pale. "It was me, Ken-ichi-*dono*," he stuttered.

Ken-ichi strode back along the hallway until he was standing in front of Ko. He towered over the younger boy, who began to tremble. "You filthy peasant," he said, his voice dangerously quiet. "How dare you insult my noble father!"

"I—I meant no insult, Ken-ichi-*dono*," Ko said.

"Whether you meant it or not, you still insulted him," Ken-ichi said. "My father is the *Jito*—and he's your lord and master. You owe him your loyalty."

Ko bowed low, his face ashen. "He has it, Ken-ichi-*dono*."

"You called him Kaminari," Ken-ichi insisted. "And

you must be punished for that!"

Ko began to tremble as Ken-ichi glared around at the other servants. "Someone fetch this peasant a sword so he can defend himself," he cried, his hand on the hilt of his own *nihonto*.

They were going to fight!

"This isn't a matter to be decided by the sword," I said, quickly stepping in front of Ko to protect him. "Ko didn't give your father the name Kaminari. He was only repeating what he heard."

Ken-ichi flushed angrily. "Who asked for your opinion, rice boy?" he snarled. "Now, get out of my way."

"No," I said firmly.

Our gazes locked and held.

There was a soft metallic whisper as Ken-ichi drew his blade, and in a heartbeat the tip was pressed against my throat. I could feel the chill steel pricking my skin.

I caught my breath, not daring to move.

A silence fell around us. From the corner of my eye, I caught a glimpse of Master Goku. He came forward and placed his hand firmly on Ken-ichi's *nihonto* blade, pushing it away from my throat.

"Sheath your sword, Ken-ichi," he said to my cousin, his voice hard and cold.

A muscle flickered in Ken-ichi's cheek, but he

didn't move. His unflinching gaze stayed locked on mine, his eyes full of hate.

Master Goku's face hardened. "You will not draw your blade against a member of my household." Goku's eyes flashed, and he raise his voice. "If there is a dispute, you will bring it to me!"

The silence around us deepened. Then slowly Ken-ichi lowered his blade and rammed it back into its sheath.

Master Goku's hard gaze swept the assembled students. "There are five days left before the great tournament that marks the end of *kenshu* training," he said. "If there is one more incident like this, any student involved will be forbidden to enter the competition."

With everything that had happened since our arrival at the dojo, I had almost forgotten about the tournament. I held my breath as the silence stretched thinly around us all. A few boys looked at the floor as if they were ashamed. Without a word, Ken-ichi turned on his heel and stalked away.

Master Goku turned to Ko and Sato. "Repeating gossip is an activity more suited to washerwomen by a stream," he said. "I expect better from servants at my dojo. Go and find something more worthy to occupy your time."

The two boys scurried away, Ko shooting me a

grateful glance over his shoulder. The other servants and students soon followed, and Hana and I were left alone with Master Goku.

"Stay out of trouble," the Master said, his voice gentle. Then he dismissed us.

As Hana and I walked away, I couldn't help thinking about how bad things had become. Uncle was starving the country and Ken-ichi's ego was raging out of control.

Master Goku was keeping him in check—just. But I wondered how long things could go on like this.

Later that night, we met up with Tatsuya for our usual practice session. He had heard from one of the other students about my encounter with Ken-ichi.

"Ken-ichi's a menace," Tatsuya said, gathering up rocks in preparation for his tea-pouring practice.

"Ko told me that Ken-ichi's already been boasting that he'll be champion of the tournament," Hana said. "He says there's no one here who's good enough to beat him."

"I might compete," I said thoughtfully. "I stand as good a chance of winning as anyone else. Ken-ichi would have to stop boasting then!" *And,* I thought, *as champion of the tournament, I would be in a good position to challenge Uncle.*

As Tatsuya and Hana began their tea-pouring practice, I perched on a nearby rock, lost in thought. Whoever became champion would be celebrated, and that honor could be used as the grounds to face Lord Hidehira openly. Uncle would not be able to refuse the challenge.

But could I win the tournament and become champion? Could I eliminate all the competition and be chosen as the best student in the school? During my time at the dojo I had put in hours of sweat and dedication. I excelled in many forms of fighting. Choji had told me recently that I was one of his best students with the *naginata* spear. Thanks to many moon phases of hard practice with the kitchen knives, I had become skillful enough to fight anyone in hand-to-hand combat with a *tanto* dagger. And my ability with a *nihonto* had improved dramatically since my swordfight with Ken-ichi at the dojo gates.

Above all, I was beginning to learn that it was not strength that mastered a blade—but precision. I knew that, with or without a weapon, I could find a weakness in every opponent.

I could do it, I told myself firmly. I could win the tournament. And once I was crowned champion, I would have proved that I could fight anybody and win. Thus would I be a worthy challenger to Uncle, and I would have my chance at revenge! My heart beat faster as I saw the way forward in my mind's eye, like a walkway lit by a shaft of bright moonlight. In five days' time I could face my uncle and avenge my father and brothers.

Above us the night sky deepened to midnight black and a faint breeze brought me the scent of blossoms. I sat quietly on my rock, as Tatsuya and Hana finished their tea pouring.

"That was much better this time," Hana told him.

"Thank you," Tatsuya said with a small bow. "Your teaching has helped, and I think I have improved. But . . ." He gave an anxious sigh. "I'm still nervous about serving tea to Goku. It's one thing doing it right during practice, but entirely different in front of the whole school and all the masters. What if my nerves get the better of me again, and I'm clumsy?"

"You won't be clumsy," Hana said firmly as she replaced the rocks around the shadow-filled garden. She took Tatsuya's hand. "You will believe in yourself, and you will remember everything you've learned here in this garden."

"I hope so," Tatsuya said quietly.

They bowed to each other in preparation for their usual sparring session. Hana was using a garden rake to defend herself from Tatsuya's *jo*.

"Higher," Tatsuya told her. "Bring your elbow up,

216

like this." He demonstrated. "And use your left foot more."

Hana stepped forward with her left foot, swung her rake, and then ducked to avoid Tatsuya's *jo*.

"Here," he said with a grin. "Swap weapons with me. I'll use the rake to show you a better hand grip. . . ."

They sparred on, swinging and cutting, weapons slicing the air. They leaped and pirouetted, using walls and rocks and even the air as stepping-stones, looking more as though they were dancing than fighting.

Tatsuya swung the garden rake again. Hana ducked once more, too late this time, and gave a little shriek as the tip of the rake swept across the top of her head. It caught in her topknot, and all at once her long hair came loose and tumbled down over her shoulders.

Horrified, she scrambled to twist it back up.

But there was too much of it! Long hair rippling in a waterfall of black silk . . .

I leaped to my feet. I had to do something before Tatsuya realized!

Tatsuya dropped the rake and stared at Hana, openmouthed.

"You're a girl!" he gasped.

CHAPTER EIGHTEEN

At last Hana managed to twist her hair up and secure it on the top of her head. "You are mistaken," she said quickly.

But Tatsuya shook his head. "I know what I saw," he insisted. "You're no more a boy than this garden rake is a lethal weapon!"

My heart was racing and I stepped forward to go to Hana.

Tatsuya quickly stopped me by barring the way with the rake. He stared into my face, a questioning look in his eyes. Across the garden, a frog jumped into the pond with a plop, the sound disturbing the stillness of the night.

"Both of you?" Tatsuya asked.

There was no use trying to convince him. We had to confess. I bit my lip and nodded.

"But why—?" he demanded.

I glanced at Hana and she gave a tiny nod. I took a deep breath and told Tatsuya the truth. "We're the daughters of Lord Yoshijiro."

Tatsuya looked astounded for a moment, then he fell to his knees in front of us and pressed his forehead to the ground.

"No!" Hana said in alarm. "Don't do that. Please get up."

Slowly Tatsuya raised his head to look at us, but he stayed on his knees. "Forgive me for any rudeness I may have shown you in the past—" he began.

But I interrupted him. "You've never been rude, Tatsuya," I said, pulling him to his feet. "And you don't have to treat us as if we're ladies of the Imperial Court. We're ordinary girls now. Our father's dead and we're in hiding."

"But why are you in hiding?" Tatsuya looked at us both, a sudden realization dawning across his face. "I remember Ken-ichi boasting to us all," he said, and gasped in horror. "Lord Hidehira's men put the household to the sword for their treachery. He said it was the custom!"

"Except that Hana and I escaped," I said quietly. "Uncle's samurai were charging through the house, smashing everything in their path, and slaughtering our servants. . . ."

Tatsuya held up a hand. "Wait," he said. "I think you'd better start at the beginning."

So Hana and I sat in a shadowy part of the rock

garden with Tatsuya, far away from prying eyes, and told him our story. We started with our real names, and then took turns describing the night at the compound when Uncle had massacred our household. One of us took up the tale when the other found it too hard to go on.

Tatsuya's face grew serious in the moonlight. Every so often his dark eyes flashed with anger.

When we reached the end of the story, he clenched one of his fists and pounded it into the palm of the other. "How dare he?" he growled. "Lord Hidehira hasn't just broken the *bushi* code; he's ripped it to shreds and trampled it into the ground!" He looked at us fiercely. "If you ever need my help . . . ," he said. "We're friends, and friends look out for one another."

"Thank you," we both said together.

Then Tatsuya gazed at us again, this time shaking his head in disbelief. "Girls," he marveled. "I still can't believe it. You know, I've never seen any girl who can fight with the skill that you two have."

"Not skilled enough, though," I said. "We must train harder." Quickly I told him my plan to win the tournament and challenge Uncle openly.

"And if I win the tournament, I will challenge the *Jito* on your and Hana's behalf," Tatsuya said, looking at me intently.

Hana looked surprised. "No, Tatsuya," she said

220

quietly. "This is our fight. We are so grateful for your friendship, but we cannot drag you into this."

I nodded in agreement. "But will you keep sparring with us?" I asked.

"Of course," he said. "Anything you need, just ask."

As the tournament drew closer, the air of excitement in the dojo intensified. The gardens and courtyards echoed with the clash of swords and *jo*. Students worked until late in the evening, calling for servants to relight the lanterns among the trees as they burned themselves out.

Choji noticed our renewed efforts and complimented us both on our improved weapons skill. "We'll make warriors of you skinny boys yet," he quipped in his gruff voice.

And every day that passed, I saw that Ken-ichi was training with the same intensity I was.

He'd taken over one of the courtyards on the far side of the school from the servants' quarters and kitchens, so at first I wasn't aware of what he was doing. But one evening, just as the sun dipped behind the curving roof of the main practice hall, Tatsuya led Hana and me along a series of walkways, through an ornamental garden to a wooden archway. As we approached, we could hear the sounds of combat—the grunts, the swiftly exhaled breaths, the impact of a fist.

"Look through the archway," Tatsuya said quietly. "This is what you're going to be up against in two days' time."

I looked, and my heart squeezed tight. Ken-ichi and his opponent, a brown-sash student called Genta, were both stripped to the waist. Their wiry bodies glistened with sweat. Surrounding them were a group of about eight or ten other students, including Ken-ichi's two friends. All eyes were fixed on Ken-ichi and Genta.

Genta circled Ken-ichi warily. One of his hands was curled loosely in front of his stomach, the other held straight out in front of him. He seemed tense, uncertain of his next move, and I could see a red mark along one of his cheekbones where Ken-ichi's fist had already struck.

My cousin, by contrast, was relaxed and alert. A half smile played around his mouth. He stepped forward and without warning unleashed a powerful punch that almost connected with Genta's jawbone. Genta quickly bent backward, swaying slightly, rolling his weight on his heels. Ken-ichi didn't wait for his recovery. He shot straight in with a hard kick, power channeling through his leg into his foot. The impact was sudden and brutal, a blow that resounded around the courtyard. I cringed as the boy's head snapped to one side, and all at once Genta was down, his face in the sand.

I saw one of Ken-ichi's friends punch the air with his fist in triumph.

Ken-ichi lowered his hands and bowed in Genta's direction—a supreme display of arrogance, for Genta was dazed and thus unable to acknowledge the supposed respect. Then, without the usual etiquette of waiting for an opponent to get up again, Ken-ichi turned to the other students. "Who's next?"

No one moved. For a moment, I thought of launching myself forward. But I stopped myself. Now was not the right time. I was beginning to learn patience.

"What, none of you?" Ken-ichi said with a sneer. "All right then, let's make it fair. I'll take on three of you. Three against one! Come on, you peasants. Who's man enough to challenge me?"

A few of the students shuffled and glanced at one another. One of Ken-ichi's friends, big and brawny, stepped forward and volunteered himself before turning and dragging forward the two students nearest to him.

Ken-ichi grinned as all three came to face him, their bare feet making tracks in the sandy floor of the courtyard. They bowed to one another as custom demanded, but Ken-ichi breached etiquette again,

223

coming up from his bow before the others had finished. They had barely gathered their wits when he launched into a punishing attack.

He is his father's son, I thought. *Ken-ichi will trample over any sacred rule in the pursuit of triumph.* I resolved to remember this fact, to know my enemy.

One of the students—quicker than the others—met him with a high block, while another moved in with a sliding foot which almost swept Ken-ichi's feet from under him. But my cousin moved fast, fists and feet flying in a blur, one move following hard on another. He caught his first attacker in the ribs, sending him toward the third attacker, who almost tripped over him. Then he ducked down to ram a shoulder into his big, brawny friend, throwing him abruptly to the ground.

The brawny boy lay flat on his back, gasping like a landed fish, while the other two students sat looking dazed.

One of the boys on the ground recovered quickly, however. He scrambled to his feet, twisted his hips, and sent a flying thrust kick at Ken-ichi's stomach. The small crowd in the courtyard winced as they heard the contact.

For a moment it looked as if Ken-ichi had met his match. He gasped and backed off for a moment, his hands clutched hard across his muscular stomach. But then he shook himself off and darted in again with a double-handed punch. His opponent ducked away at the last minute and launched into another devastating kick.

But Ken-ichi was expecting it this time. He caught the kick in midair before it had time to connect, trapping the ankle between his arm and his ribs. He twisted his body, forcing his opponent off balance. Instantly the boy collapsed to the ground, locked into an awkward position by Ken-ichi's painful control over his leg.

"Stop!" the boy yelped.

"Do you yield?" Ken-ichi demanded through gritted teeth.

"Yes . . . I yield," the boy gasped in pain.

"Then I declare myself the champion!" Abruptly Ken-ichi let go and the boy fell to the ground, clutching his ankle. A couple of other students ran to help him up, and he limped across the courtyard.

"Can't you walk away like a true warrior?" Ken-ichi sneered at him. "A twisted ankle is hardly a major injury. I was holding back—if I'd wanted to, I could have snapped your leg like a twig!"

The boy flushed red with shame.

Out of sight of Ken-ichi, as the boy limped passed, I asked, "Are you all right?"

"I think so," the boy replied, but he was breathing hard.

"Choji has some medical supplies in the kitchen,"

I told him. "Why don't you go and have your ankle bandaged?"

As his friends helped the injured boy away, I stood up and looked at Tatsuya.

"Seen enough?" he asked in a low voice.

"Yes," I said.

I *had* seen enough. I knew now that my cousin was a deadly opponent, skilled and ruthless.

I also knew that if this had been a full-contact bout instead of a practice, then it was almost certain that Ken-ichi's opponent would never have walked again.

The night before the tournament, everyone gathered in the main practice hall for one last formal tea ceremony. The period of intensive *kenshu* training was over.

"This evening," Master Goku said, "I would like every student to take a turn at pouring tea for the *cha no yoriai.*"

Ken-ichi was chosen to go first, and he approached the low lacquered table with his usual confidence. He wore a crisp fresh kimono and neat black *hakama* trousers, his hair greased and folded on top of his head. With his handsome face and calm self-assurance, he looked every inch the noble samurai, and Master Goku acknowledged him with a bow. He bowed, kneeled, and ladled out the tea perfectly.

"Your technique is excellent, Ken-ichi," the Master said. "You are a credit to your father."

Ken-ichi walked back to his place, looking at his classmates as if they were already his subjects. One by one, the other students followed him. Each one bowed, kneeled, poured.

When it was Tatsuya's turn, Hana and I watched apprehensively. Tatsuya had worked so hard to improve, but what if, as he feared, his nerves took over when he was under pressure?

We needn't have worried. Tatsuya was perfection itself. Poised and calm, his movements spare and precise, he could have served *cha* to the Emperor himself and been praised for it.

Master Goku bowed to Tatsuya. "You have particularly pleased me," the Master said. "You have not only shown great improvement, but also the unshakeable will to be the best. And the best is what you have become tonight, Tatsuya."

Tatsuya blushed and bowed low. Master Goku smiled. "You have the focus and passion of a true samurai, my son."

I felt my heart swell with pride that Tatsuya had reached his goal. I knew that I still had my own challenge to fulfill. I still had to kick down the willow tree.

As Tatsuya returned to his seat, threading a pathway through the other students, I saw Ken-ichi roll his eyes. But Tatsuya was oblivious, smiling happily. Although he could not publicly acknowledge our help in his perfect tea-pouring skills, he bowed slightly to Hana and me as he passed.

Later that night, the three of us meditated together in the rock garden. We didn't want to spar, preferring instead to save our energies for the next day's tournament. I felt as if our time at the dojo had all been leading up to this.

Tatsuya sat in tranquil isolation in a far corner of the garden, his dark hair made silver by the moonlight. Hana was kneeling, eyes closed, face serene.

I kneeled motionless in a pool of light shed by a nearby lantern. My spirit felt calm, my whole inner being focused. For a moment I gazed across the rock garden to where the willow's sad dead branches swept low to the ground. The moment had come.

A breeze stirred my hair. I got up and slowly walked across the moonlit garden to the willow tree. I positioned myself carefully, adjusting my balance as I took a wide-legged stance. My knees were soft, my hands curled one in front of the other near my stomach.

Standing very still, I closed my eyes.

Count your breaths, Kimi . . . , Master Goku's voice seemed to echo inside my mind. *Breathe in, two, three, four . . . breathe out, two, three, four . . .*

I focused on my breathing and let conscious thought slip away. Memories faded.

Something happened then. A great emptiness seemed to fill me, abruptly replaced by a vital force that pushed up from the depths of my soul. Power surged through me. My limbs hummed with energy.

Eyes flashing open, I unleashed a fierce *yokogeri* kick, channeling every ounce of vigor and weight through my leg and into my foot. My heel hit the trunk of the willow like a blacksmith's hammer. A loud *crack!* echoed through the night—

I leaped back just in time as the trunk snapped. And then the tree was falling! Branches whipped the air and at last the dead willow tree went crashing to the ground.

Hana and Tatsuya came running across the rock garden, bursting with excitement and exclamations of wonder. "You did it! You really did it!"

I stared at the toppled tree and smiled. "I think I'm ready."

CHAPTER NINETEEN

At last the day of the tournament dawned. The first day of *Seimei*, true to the weather prophets, was clear and bright. I could hardly believe how long Hana and I had been at the dojo. I stood at the gap in the screens of our tiny bedroom and gazed out across the gardens and courtyards, rubbing the sleep from my eyes as I thought about Mother and Moriyasu. Had Goku found them? He hadn't said anything, but I knew that if anyone could find them, Goku could.

The air was warmer now. Spring was really here and the cherry blossom trees were in glorious full bloom. I could see across the walkways and low walls to the main gates of the school. They had been opened wide and even this early in the day there was a steady stream of people arriving for the tournament—farmers from the neighboring villages rubbed shoulders with merchants and craftsmen, local samurai families hurried in the wake of powerful lords carried on gilded palanquins.

By midmorning there was a festival atmosphere around the fight arena, which had been set up in the main courtyard. Those without the privilege of shaded seats laughed and joked as they jostled for places on long wooden benches. Snack sellers hawked their wares and a few peasants in ragged jackets sold tiny wooden figures that had been painted to look as though they were wearing the brown kimono and black *hakama* trousers of the dojo. "Buy your champions!" the woodcarvers cried. "Buy your champions here!"

"Are you nervous, Kimi?" Hana asked, as we helped each other to dress for combat, lacing on shoulder guards and leather sleeve armor.

"A little." I slung my sword from my sash, beside Moriyasu's little wooden *bokken*, which I was wearing as a good-luck charm. "Are you?"

She shook her head. "We've worked hard and done all we can to prepare. Winning or losing is out of our hands now."

"I just hope I've done enough," I said grimly, but my words were drowned out by the sudden blare of conch-shell trumpets announcing the arrival of the *Jito*.

"He's here," Hana whispered.

"Tatsuya says Uncle will be the one to judge each

round of the tournament and choose the champion," I told her. "I can't help thinking that gives Kenichi an unfair advantage."

"Uncle is not interested in what is fair," Hana agreed. "And neither is our cousin."

As we made our way along the walkway, my heart began to pound with excitement and anticipation. At last, the time had come for Hana and me to put our hard work and practice to the test. I could hear the excitement of the crowd as I neared the main courtyard, and as I turned the corner I saw rows and rows of eager faces.

The whole school had gathered, along with half the province, it seemed. Hundreds of people filled the wooden benches that lined the huge square fight arena. The competing students were kneeling in rows near the first fight area. Among them were servants and peasants from the village, all treated as equals today.

Some of the boys looked anxious; others were lost in quiet contemplation as they prepared their minds for the combat ahead. One of the young masters was walking around the edge of the fight arena, checking that the ground was even and that the white raked underfoot had been neatly swept.

Uncle was sitting up on a high wooden platform, shaded by a lacquered paper parasol. He was wearing formal dress, his red and gold robes arranged around him in flowing folds. Two swords glimmered at his waist. Beside him sat Master Goku, his face impassive.

Tatsuya joined us as Hana and I made our way toward the rows of competitors. He was dressed for combat in leather armor, his *jo* in his hand. He seemed to have gained a new confidence since the *cha no yoriai* last night. He walked with his head held high, drawing glances of admiration from people in the crowd.

As we moved between the rows of merchants and farm workers, I realized I could hear them whispering about the new *Jito*.

"I hear he's gathering weapons," muttered a skinny man.

"Breaking alliances across the kingdom," said another.

"He's half the man his brother was," agreed a wrinkled old woman, cooling herself with a painted paper fan.

I took strength from the knowledge that the people hadn't forgotten my father.

The crowd shifted around us, murmuring, and we came to an area that was roped off with lengths of silk. Men and women in expensive-looking kimonos were seated under a long billowing canopy, which

233

shaded them from the sun. Servants in plain blue jackets and trousers served them tea in beautiful porcelain bowls, and I even recognized a few of them as visitors in my father's household. These were important local families, friends of the *Jito*.

As I passed by with Hana and Tatsuya, a hand suddenly reached out and touched my sleeve.

Surprised, I turned around—and found myself looking directly into the face of Miura no Megumi, one of my mother's oldest friends. She was as tall and elegant as a willow tree in her green silk kimono, her red-painted lips curved in a friendly smile.

My heart began to pound with fear.

"Don't I know you, child?" she asked me.

"N-no," I stuttered, trying to deepen my voice to sound more boyish.

"Oh, but we have met before," she insisted, her dark eyes twinkling with good humor. "I just can't remember where . . . wait, it will come to me in a moment. . . ."

All at once, Tatsuya stepped forward. "Forgive me, dear lady," he said in a pompous voice that sounded remarkably like Ken-ichi. "This boy is my servant. He's a lowly peasant from a northern province. I am sure a lady of your standing cannot have met him before."

He bowed deeply and respectfully, and then smiled up at her. "I, however, am delighted to make your acquaintance." He puffed himself up importantly, looking more and more like Ken-ichi with every moment. "May I introduce myself? I am Lord Fujiwara. . . ."

As he uttered the word *Lord*, Tatsuya shot me a look that seemed to say, *Get out of here, now!* My mother's friend, meanwhile, seemed impressed at finding herself face to face with such a young lord. As she bowed low to Tatsuya, Hana and I hurriedly slipped away through the crowd.

"Thank goodness Tatsuya's mind is as fast as the arrows he fires," Hana whispered.

"We should have been prepared for something like that to happen," I said, biting my lip in frustration. "We could have ruined everything just then. No more mistakes. This is the chance we've been waiting for!"

At last we reached the area where the other competing students and servants were kneeling. We saw Ko sitting with Sato, Genta, and the boy who'd injured his ankle during the bout with Ken-ichi. Farther away sat my cousin himself, oozing confidence and flanked by his two friends. He sneered as he saw Tatsuya hurry to join us.

"I think I convinced her," Tatsuya said to me in a low voice.

"That you were a lord?" I said with a smile. "I should think so—you almost convinced me!"

He grinned back at me. "No . . . ," he said, looking embarrassed. "I think I convinced her that you were beneath her notice. But I'd keep out of her way, just in case."

We kneeled down together with Hana. I closed my eyes, allowing my heartbeat to settle as I composed myself and summoned the energy that had consumed me the previous night.

On the raised platform, Master Goku kneeled before the crowd and spread his arms wide. "I would like to welcome everyone to our tournament today," he said. Turning to Uncle, he bowed low. "We are honored to have the presence of our new *Jito*, Lord Hidehira."

Hidehira smiled thinly and bowed back, red and gold robes rippling.

"Many of you," Goku went on, turning back to the crowd, "have come great distances to witness acts of incredible courage and skill. I have seen these boys in training and I guarantee that you will not be disappointed." He gazed down at the students, folding his hands into his wide sleeves. "You will all fight honorably, as your training dictates." The students all bowed their heads respectfully. Goku smiled and straightened up, his gaze sweeping the crowd once more. "Let the combat commence!" he exclaimed.

We all bowed to the *Jito*, though I hated every

moment of it. If it wouldn't draw immediate rebuke and attention, I would have refused. Next, we bowed to Master Goku, and I did it with sincerity and humility.

The competitors turned and formed a circle facing inward, and we all bowed to one another to show respect. Then the tournament had begun.

My first fight went well. I was matched with Sato, who I had seen fighting with Ko a number of times. I knew his moves and was able to anticipate his low strikes and easily block his high slices. Soon I had him pinned to the sandy ground, my knee against his chest and the flat of my knife held against his throat. He slapped the ground twice to show that he submitted. Mister Choji was the referee and he held my arm high as the crowd applauded my win. I glanced toward the platform where Uncle was sitting. He was far away and I could only see the color of his robes, but with each successive win, I knew I would move closer.

Soon it was Hana's turn to fight. She won her first bout against a village boy easily, and then drew Tatsuya as her opponent in the *jo* round in the first fight area in front of the *Jito*. I hoped that Uncle would not recognize her, but I knew with Hana's swift fighting movements, he would have a hard time getting a good look. Silence settled on the arena as the fighters bowed to each other and to the *Jito*, then they took their places.

I watched as Hana let her weight settle evenly on both feet, centering herself. She held the wooden staff with both hands, her grip loose and easy, ready to slide along the shaft if necessary. She stared across the arena at Tatsuya. They measured each other for a moment.

Abruptly Hana attacked, letting out a yell as she ran forward and brought her *jo* down hard. Tatsuya blocked her, and the two weapons knocked loudly. Twisting, Hana swiftly jabbed the end of her *jo* at Tatsuya's stomach. Her feet slid through the white sand, moving quickly. Tatsuya deflected and danced around her, catching a glancing blow on the end of her *jo*.

They brought their weapons back close to their bodies for a moment and stepped around each other warily. They both rolled their wrists as they squared up again, their weapons twirling in front of them.

Tatsuya attacked suddenly, his *jo* spinning as he brought it down. Hana swiftly brought the *jo* over her head to block him, keeping her feet in a strong stance. A terrible clash tore the air, and I could see her arms were jarred.

I bit my lip, willing her on as she pirouetted, shifting her hands along the polished wooden shaft to lunge again, feet dancing. But Tatsuya was quick. He moved in close and pushed one end of the *jo* behind one of Hana's legs. With a quick twist of his wrist, he buckled Hana at the knee.

Half kneeling, she grunted, her center of balance gone, and it was easy for Tatsuya to take her weapon from her. Hana had no choice but to concede.

Choji stepped into the arena and declared Tatsuya the winner, holding his arm high. The crowd cheered and applauded, some of the younger students putting their fingers to their mouths and whistling. I was torn—pleased for Tatsuya that he had won his bout, but devastated to see Hana out of the tournament.

Hana, however, was smiling and that made me feel a little better. She and Tatsuya bowed good-naturedly to each other and then turned to bow toward the *Jito* and Master Goku.

"Just wait until we fight hand to hand," Hana teased him as they resumed their positions next to me.

"I think I would struggle to compete with your silent fists," he responded with a warm smile.

I fought again and again, beating boys who were older and more experienced than I. The crowd seemed to enjoy the fact that a servant was winning. They hammered their fists on the wooden benches and hooted their approval. On the other side of the courtyard, I could hear the crowd cheering on Ken-ichi's victories as well.

The sun moved higher across the sky. Gradually, through the morning, student after student was eliminated from the tournament, until just six remained. Tatsuya, Ken-ichi, and I were among them.

Slowly an expectant hush fell on the crowd, and Master Goku stood up.

"Friends and students," he said. "This morning you have witnessed deeds of great skill. You have looked into the faces of future samurai and seen passion, discipline, and steely determination." A buzz of agreement rose from the crowd. "The final round of combat will be a *ya-awase*, or archery duel, and we ask our great *Jito*, Lord Hidehira, to do us the honor of judging which contestant is the most skilled with a longbow."

I saw Ken-ichi look up in shock, and then shoot a furious glance at Tatsuya. Archery was Ken-ichi's weak point, whereas we had all seen Tatsuya split arrow after arrow. And I had been training with the longbow, under Tatsuya's direction, for many phases of the moon.

I closed my eyes for a moment and prayed for a steady hand.

Hana helped me to strap a leather protector onto

my forearm and a quiver of arrows across my back. "You can do this, Kimi," she said softly. "Focus." Her voice dropped to a whisper, and she added, "Do it for Moriyasu."

We all bowed in the direction of Master Goku and Lord Hidehira. Again, I gritted my teeth at having to bow to my treacherous uncle. Then we turned to make our way out into the middle of the fight area. I could see Ken-ichi in the middle of our little group. He was slightly behind Tatsuya, his shoulders broad beneath his leather shoulder padding. All around us, the crowd bubbled with excitement and a few of the younger students shouted encouragement.

Without warning, Ken-ichi's foot flashed out in front of Tatsuya and suddenly Tatsuya was falling. He tried to save himself by putting out his hand, but his body collapsed awkwardly and his arm bore the whole weight of the fall. As he landed, he cried out, the harsh sound echoing around the courtyard, and kneeled very still, clasping his shoulder. His face was white with pain.

Instantly Ken-ichi bowed apologetically. "So sorry," he said. "How clumsy of me!"

Clumsy? I thought in a blaze of anger as I hurried across to crouch at Tatsuya's side. Ken-ichi was never clumsy. This had been something else. He'd hated it last night when Master Goku said Tatsuya was the most improved student at the dojo. Terrified that Tatsuya might beat him in the archery competition, Ken-ichi had obviously decided to eliminate him. He certainly was his father's son.

"Are you all right?" I whispered to Tatsuya.

He shook his head. "My shoulder is in agony," he muttered through clenched teeth.

I tried to help him sit more comfortably. Around us, the crowd had been still for a moment. But now a few people hissed their disapproval at Ken-ichi.

"Dishonorable conduct!" a man in blue silk robes exclaimed.

Ken-ichi glanced up, swept the crowd with his arrogant gaze. "What?" he cried. "Surely you don't think—?" Disbelief swept across his face and he held his hands wide, palms upward, the picture of injured innocence. "It was an accident!"

But I didn't believe him, nor did the crowd. As a couple of older students hurried out to help Tatsuya out of the arena, a few people in the audience began to thump rhythmically on their wooden benches. A restless muttering began to buzz through the air.

I heard a farmer say, "That was clearly deliberate," while a woman cried, "Sabotage!"

Master Goku slowly walked forward to the edge

of the platform and raised his hands for silence. A muscle flickered in his cheek as he stared down at Ken-ichi. I straightened up, holding my breath. Was my cousin going to get away with his behavior? The thought made me boil up in outrage.

"I saw what you did, and it was no accident," Master Goku said to Ken-ichi. "You have deliberately injured a fellow student and prevented him from competing. This action brings dishonor upon yourself and upon the dojo." He folded his hands inside his sleeves. "Therefore, you are disqualified from this tournament. Please step out of the arena, Ken-ichi."

Relief swept through me. This was justice.

"No!" Ken-ichi cried, stepping toward the platform. "That's not fair. . . ."

But Master Goku stood firm. "Step out of the arena, Ken-ichi," he said again.

Ken-ichi stayed where he was, a rebellious expression on his face. "I'm the *Jito*'s son," he said. "No one can stop me from competing. Not even you, Sensei." He turned to look at Lord Hidehira. "Father," he appealed. "Tell him—"

Lord Hidehira stared down at his son. His dark eyes glittered like black ice. "I will tell him nothing!" he snapped. "You are a fool, Ken-ichi. A stupid, childish puppy!"

Ken-ichi turned white with horror. "Father, I beg you!"

Lord Hidehira ignored him and turned to Master Goku. "A thousand apologies for this boy's conduct, Master Goku. Punish him as you see fit." Both men bowed low to each other, and when Hidehira straightened up his face was tightly controlled. He faced Master Goku for a moment longer, then he said, "I regret that I can no longer be the judge of this tournament because I have been shamed by the conduct of my son. I must leave now, and beg your forgiveness for any loss of face that Ken-ichi has brought upon your dojo."

I gazed in astonishment at Lord Hidehira as he swept across the platform, down the steps, and toward a troop of waiting samurai. My heart sank hopelessly as I realized my plan to challenge him openly had been foiled. Heads turned as the crowd watched him go, a breathless silence falling on the assembly. I caught Hana's eye. She was standing at the edge of the competitors' waiting area, her fists clenched as she watched the scene unfold. I wanted to go stand with her, but I didn't dare draw attention to myself.

Ken-ichi stayed where he was for a moment, then suddenly he launched himself forward, running after his father. "Father!" he cried. "Don't leave! What happened was right and just. That boy, Tatsuya, is a peasant! You've always said that the peasants should be kept in their place. . . ."

Lord Hidehira wheeled around and glared at his son. "Your behavior would shame a peasant," he said, his voice tight with fury. "You have heaped shame upon me and disgraced the name of Yamamoto. From this day, you are no longer the son of the *Jito*!"

A gasp went up from the crowd. Hana and I exchanged a startled glance.

Ken-ichi gaped at his father in horror. "No!" he cried. But it was too late. In a swirl of red and gold robes, Uncle disappeared into the midst of his waiting soldiers.

Desperate, Ken-ichi stumbled forward, but the ranks of samurai closed behind his father, hands on the hilts of their swords. I had no doubt that they would cut him down if they had to.

There was a moment of shocked silence, and then Ken-ichi wheeled around to stare at Master Goku. "This is your fault!" he said, his lips white with fury. "You did this . . . you accepted that stinking peasant into this school. He should never have been allowed to train among us."

"All students are equal," Master Goku said, and he began to turn away. "Calm yourself, Ken-ichi."

"I will not be calm," Ken-ichi spluttered. Leaping up the steps and onto the platform, he stood eye to eye with Master Goku. "I challenge you!" he said fiercely. "I challenge you to fight me, Sensei."

The crowd gasped. A challenge like that, once issued, could not be retracted. Astounded, I stared up at Ken-ichi. Hana put her hand up to her mouth.

One of the students beside me shook his head. "No one has challenged the Master for years," he muttered.

"I do not accept your challenge," Master Goku said.

"You must," Ken-ichi said staunchly. "I know the code of the *bushi*. No honorable challenge can be refused!"

There was silence for a moment; then Master Goku bowed. "So be it," he said, so quietly that I had to strain my ears to hear him. "But I urge you to allow a period of reflection and conversation before we choose our weapons. Will you come with me to the meditation room?"

Ken-ichi hesitated for a moment. "Very well," he said at last. "But don't imagine that you're going to talk me out of this duel. I fight for the honor of this school and the right to be educated with my own kind—not with filthy peasants!"

"I hear what you say," Master Goku said. With a

sweep of his long robes, he made his way down from the platform and out of the courtyard.

Ken-ichi followed behind him, but as he drew near to Choji he growled at the head servant, "Bring us some *cha.*"

Choji glanced at Master Goku, his eyebrows raised as if unsure whether he should take orders from the disowned son of the *Jito.*

Master Goku nodded. "Tea will refresh us," he said quietly. "Thank you, Choji."

As they left the courtyard, the crowd stirred restlessly. Choji signaled to me. "Take the tea to the meditation room, Kagenashi," he said. "And stay with Sensei in case he needs anything else."

I hurried across to Hana, who helped me unlace my sleeve armor and shoulder guards. "Ken-ichi doesn't know what he's doing," she whispered. "It's madness to challenge Master Goku!"

My mind was in turmoil. The tournament was in chaos, and so was my plan to win and face Uncle openly.

By the time I got to the meditation room, Ken-ichi and Master Goku were kneeling opposite each other. I bowed and approached the table with my tray of drinking bowls. Master Goku seemed hardly to notice me. He was composed and calm, his gaze resting lightly on Ken-ichi's face. By contrast, my

247

cousin simmered with rage. His shoulders were tense, his fists clenched.

I set the tray on the table between them, bowed, and withdrew to a corner of the room to wait.

"Ken-ichi, please pour the *cha*," Master Goku said.

"The student must serve the Master," Ken-ichi muttered. His lip curled. "You're thinking that perhaps this will calm me down. Well, it won't, Sensei. Someone has to stand up for honor, duty, and tradition, and if I'm to be the one—so be it!"

"You speak so freely of such ideals," Master Goku said gently. "But you forget that a samurai is also bound by other rules. He must be humble; he must control his pride; and above all he must show tolerance of his fellow men." He watched as Ken-ichi reached out to put green tea powder into the bowls. "I'm sorry that your father spoke so angrily to you. Would you like me to intercede?"

"No!" Ken-ichi's hands shook and the sleeves of his kimono fluttered across the rims of the tea bowls, almost tipping them. "I don't want you to do anything on my behalf, Sensei. We will fight, and then my father will see that I'm worthy to be his son once more . . . and my honor will be restored!" As he said this, Ken-ichi caught Master Goku's gaze with his own and held it. His usual grace and elegance seemed to have deserted him, and his hands fumbled clumsily as he added more tea to the bowls.

He's nervous, I thought. *More than nervous, he's frightened.* But that was hardly surprising. Ken-ichi had challenged Master Goku to a duel—a duel he would certainly lose.

I gazed at my cousin sadly. There was no honor to be gained from fighting the Master.

"Your father would think you a worthy son if you behaved like a samurai," Master Goku said. "Accept responsibility for your actions. Apologize to Tatsuya, and put this episode behind you."

"Apologize to that peasant?" Ken-ichi spat. "Never!" He picked up a tea bowl and held it between his fingers, offering to Master Goku. "Drink your *cha,* Sensei. And we'll toast your good health."

Master Goku accepted the tea bowl, bowed, and sipped. "This is a little bitter, Ken-ichi. Too much powder perhaps?"

Ken-ichi shrugged, watching as Master Goku sipped again. "Perhaps," he said. "Or perhaps you taste the bile of your own disappointment, Sensei. It must be galling to have had your precious tournament cut short."

"I am disappointed with you, Ken-ichi. Nothing else," Master Goku said. He sipped again and then drained the bowl. "I give you one last chance to change your mind about the duel."

Ken-ichi shook his head and scrambled to his feet, his tea untouched.

"A samurai never changes his mind," he said. I knew that there was no going back when Ken-ichi spoke again. "Choose your weapon, Sensei!"

CHAPTER TWENTY

M aster Goku sighed. "If you insist, Ken-ichi. I choose the *yari* spear, an ancient and noble weapon of the battlefield." With that, he rose to his feet and led Ken-ichi out of the meditation room.

I paused to quickly tidy the table, wiping the tea bowls clean. One of them had green, gritty residue at the bottom and I frowned. How strange—green tea powder didn't usually leave a residue. . . . I sniffed the bowl, noticing a bitter smell.

Perhaps the green tea wasn't very good quality? Who knew where it was coming from, what with all the food shortages since Uncle took over as *Jito*.

I stacked the bowls carefully, leaving the table neat before I hurried back outside.

In the fight arena, the crowd seemed to have grown larger, as though word had spread outside the dojo and people were coming from nearby to witness the duel between Master and student.

As they went to get their weapons, I hurried back to my place and found Tatsuya sitting with Hana, who was massaging his shoulder through his kimono. Ko was kneeling beside them.

"Are you badly hurt?" I asked Tatsuya.

He shook his head. "I must have sprained my shoulder when I landed awkwardly. It hurts, but it's nothing that a few days' rest won't fix."

Down in the arena, Master Goku was taking off his flowing ceremonial robes and handing them to Choji. Soon he was wearing just an undershirt and breeches, his feet bare on the sandy floor of the courtyard. Ken-ichi stood facing him, looking bulky in his shoulder armor and leather arm protectors. He was dressed for archery, not close combat.

"Surely it's not fair for Ken-ichi to wear so much armor," I muttered as Choji brought forward their *yari*.

"Don't worry," Tatsuya reassured me. "the Master knows what he's doing. No armor means he's lighter on his feet. He'll be able to dance around Ken-ichi and tire him out."

The spears were perhaps four feet long, the type usually carried into battle by samurai on horseback. Each had a wooden shaft covered in lacquered bamboo strips, wrapped in wire at intervals with a heavy steel pommel at the blunt end. The blades were straight, flat, steel daggers, razor sharp for cutting and stabbing.

A murmur rose from the crowd and people edged closer to the fight arena, keen to get a good view.

The crowd fell silent as the two combatants bowed and took up their fighting stances. Master Goku's gaze was steady, watching Ken-ichi alertly . . . and then the fight began.

Ken-ichi lunged forward, spear glittering in the sunshine. Master Goku blocked, and the clash of iron blades tore the air. Then Ken-ichi was leaping sideways, lunging again, and then again. Master Goku defended with skill and speed, using his body in harmony with the spear. His torso weaved back and forth as he met every move with an expert deflection.

Around me the men and women in the crowd gasped and sighed as Ken-ichi unleashed one stinging attack after another, his spear whirling, his arms flashing like the spokes of a wheel. I clenched my fists, watching intently.

My cousin was as skillful with a *yari* as he had been with his sword that day I had fought him outside the gates of the dojo. But it could never be enough to best his teacher.

Master Goku began to move faster, his feet kicking up arcs of white sand. The noise from the crowd intensified and expanded, breaking in a wave against the stone walls of the courtyard.

Goku deflected each one of Ken-ichi's attempts and did not once try to attack his student. the Master's superior skill was clear for all to see.

How would this fight end? Ken-ichi looked like he would never give up, but surely Goku wouldn't really injure Ken-ichi. . . .

But then, Ken-ichi flexed his knees, coming in with a low slice that only just missed Goku's stomach. My heart began to beat harder.

"Ken-ichi seems to be getting closer to a strike," I murmured to Hana.

She bit her lip, her gaze fixed on Master Goku. Abruptly she reached sideways and grabbed my sleeve. "Something's wrong!" Her voice was a low and urgent whisper.

"What do you mean?" I asked. My fists were clenched so tight that I could feel my nails driving into my palms as I watched Goku swing into a sudden attack.

But my sister shook her head. "Watch Sensei," she said. "He's slower than usual."

I followed her gaze and at first I couldn't see what she meant. Master Goku's spear sliced sideways and upward. He was driving Ken-ichi relentlessly backward. A murmur of voices rose from the crowd. Some of the students leaped to their feet, yelling encouragement to Master Goku. Nobody seemed to be cheering for Ken-ichi, who was buckling under the onslaught. Everything about his movements spoke of defeat.

But then Goku missed a beat. Instead of striking into Ken-ichi's center, Goku's jab went wide.

Ken-ichi took the advantage and struck back, the shaft of his spear clanging against Goku's. They struck and parried, struck again, and I saw that Master Goku *was* slowing down, as though his limbs were suddenly too heavy. A strange look washed across his face. He frowned in confusion, brought his spear up to catch a glancing blow from Ken-ichi, and shook his head as if to clear it.

"He looks like one of Father's samurai looks after drinking too much sake," Hana murmured.

Master Goku stepped forward to attack again, missed his footing, and slumped to one knee. Hana was right. He looked like he was drunk. *What was wrong with him?*

The crowd gasped, and someone yelled, "Come on, Sensei! On your feet."

"What's the matter, Master?" Ken-ichi taunted loudly. "Getting too *old* to fight a mere student?"

In the arena, Ken-ichi danced toward Master Goku, launching a sudden, vicious kick that knocked the Master to the ground.

"Get up!" Tatsuya called urgently.

But Master Goku lay there on his back in the sand, looking dazed. Ken-ichi stood over him for a moment. "Do you yield?" he asked, his voice tight.

The crowd waited breathlessly, and at last Master Goku shook his head. "I will never yield to you." He rolled sideways and came up onto his knees, then launched a sluggish attack with his spear. Ken-ichi parried it effortlessly. Goku's momentum sent him stumbling to the ground.

"Do you yield?" Ken-ichi demanded again, aiming his spear at the Master. His voice was louder this time, as if he was sure of victory and he wanted everyone to know it.

"Never!" Master Goku said again. Pain and fatigue were etched across his face and suddenly he looked like an old man. His gaze slipped sideways and for a heartbeat, his eyes made contact with mine.

This isn't right, I thought. Suddenly my mind raced back to that day up behind the bathhouse, when Ken-ichi had talked about slipping poison into drinks.

My skin prickled with dread. Hadn't there been a gritty residue in the bottom of the tea bowls when I wiped them?

And hadn't Master Goku complained of the *cha* tasting bitter?

Ken-ichi must have poisoned him!

I launched myself forward, desperately elbowing through the crowd to get to Master Goku. People got in my way, pushing at me in confusion. "Please," I begged, my voice raw and savage. "Let me through."

Through the press of the crowd I could see the Master struggling to rise to his feet once more. His movements were listless and heavy, but his face was stubborn. I knew in my heart that he would keep on getting up until whatever it was that Ken-ichi had put in his *cha* finally stopped his heart beating.

Ken-ichi knocked Master Goku down for a third time. Caught between two farmers, I watched as my cousin reached down and wrenched the Master's spear from his grasp.

He flipped it over, and then held the point lightly to Master Goku's chest. "Yield," he said.

"No." Goku was panting for breath now, his face the color of ash and his lips blue. He reached up and gripped the spear's shining blade. "You have not won this fight fairly, Ken-ichi—"

"Silence!" Ken-ichi roared. "And yield to my honorable victory!"

"There is no honor left in you," Goku gasped, and I could see panic spread across Ken-ichi's face. "You have—"

Before the Master could say another word, my cousin brought his *yari* spear plunging down.

"No!" I yelled, and shoved the people in front of me out of the way with all my strength. As I broke through the crowd, my spirit broke once again.

Ken-ichi had stabbed Master Goku through the heart.

CHAPTER TWENTY-ONE

Crimson blood seeped out around the blade and darkened Master Goku's white shirt. Behind me, Hana let out an anguished cry. I turned to see her rushing forward. She seemed to fly past me through the stunned crowed, her gaze fixed on Goku.

Finally the crowd parted for me and I fell to my knees at Hana's side in the dirt of the courtyard. Master Goku's eyes were closed, and there was a trickle of blood at one corner of his mouth.

Hana kneeled too and slid her hand under his head. "Sensei," she whispered urgently. "Sensei, don't leave us."

All around us, people crowded in close. I was aware of Choji leaning over us. "Sensei, open your eyes," he pleaded, his voice hoarse with distress.

Master Goku's eyes fluttered open. He glanced first at Hana and then at me. "S-silent Fist," he whispered. "And Shadowless Feet . . ." His face twisted and pain seemed to overwhelm him for a moment.

Behind him, Ken-ichi dropped his *yari* spear. "It . . . it was only supposed to slow him down," he muttered. He looked suddenly like the little boy who I'd played with all those years ago.

I turned back to see Master Goku struggling to speak.

Hana was shaking her head. "Please, please don't leave us."

"Beneath the cherry blossoms," he said to me with a groan, gripping Hana's hand tightly. "Look beneath the cherry blossoms. . . ."

Still kneeling at his side, I glanced across the courtyard to the cherry blossom trees that lined the walls. A slight breeze stirred their branches and the pink and white petals began to fall to the ground, as if the trees were weeping.

"What do you mean?" I asked him. "Look for what beneath the cherry blossoms?"

Master Goku's gaze fixed on mine as he struggled to take a breath. His chest rose, then fell . . . and was still. His eyes widened, staring up at the sky, and I saw that he would never tell us what he meant about the cherry blossoms.

"He's dead," Choji said in disbelief. "Sensei is dead. May the Buddha bless him and give him peace."

A woman in the crowd made a shocked sound, and an old man nearby bowed his head in sorrow. I felt my throat go so tight that I could hardly breathe. Hana let out a muffled sob and leaned forward until her forehead was touching Master Goku's shoulder.

I glanced up to see that Ken-ichi was motionless. His face was as white as the sand beneath his feet. He caught me looking at him and opened his mouth to speak, but no words came out.

I stood up. "Murderer!"

"I—I didn't mean to," he stammered.

"Yes, you did," I cried. "You had every intention of killing him or you wouldn't have *poisoned* him!"

A shocked gasp rose from the crowd.

"Poison?" Choji said, looking up at me in surprise.

"This slave has gone mad," Ken-ichi said quickly. "He's babbling. He doesn't know what he's talking about. How ridiculous, to accuse the son of the *Jito*!"

I shook my head. "You poisoned him," I said firmly, narrowing my eyes as I studied my cousin. How could I prove it? Did he still have the poison on him? The only place he could have possibly hidden it was . . .

His sash.

In one fluid movement I drew my sword and

sliced it downward across Ken-ichi's knotted belt. With a whisper, the fabric parted and dropped to the floor.

A tiny black leather pouch landed at Ken-ichi's feet.

In a heartbeat, Choji had snatched up the pouch and loosened the drawstring. When he took his fingers out, the tips were covered in a fine green powder.

"That's nothing!" Ken-ichi said. "Just a little ground seaweed to flavor the soup at lunchtime. . . ."

Choji sniffed the powder and frowned. "Ground seaweed, you say? Then you won't mind tasting it, will you?" and he thrust his fingers under Ken-ichi's nose.

Ken-ichi went even paler and I thought for a moment that he was going to faint. He stared at Choji for a moment. All around us the crowd shifted restlessly.

"No," he said at last. "I won't taste it. I'm the son of the *Jito* and you'll have to take my word for it."

"Your word doesn't count for much," I said sharply. "For you are no longer the son of the *Jito*. Remember?"

Ken-ichi shot me a venomous look. "Shut up, rice boy," he snarled. "I knew you were trouble. I should have cut you down the day you first showed your

262

filthy peasant face at the gates of the dojo!"

My sword was still in my hand and I leaped at Ken-ichi with a yell of blind fury. He just had time to draw his own blade and defend himself before I was slicing at him again. He knew he was not fighting for the title of champion anymore, or his honor. He was fighting for his life. Everything that I had held back since my father's murder came surging up through me in a torrent of rage and fury. I could feel power humming through my sword arm.

Ken-ichi buckled beneath my attack. But my anger made me clumsy. In a moment he recovered himself and came back at me, spinning and slicing, his nimble feet dancing back and forth. He leaped sideways, then twisted his body, bringing his sword downward in a glittering arc.

Gasping, I ducked backward, only just able to get out of the way of his blade. . . .

Emotion is the ally of your opponent. I could almost hear Goku's voice drift into my head. A breeze stirred the blossom trees on the far side of the courtyard, releasing another shower of petals, and all at once I felt a great calm descend upon me. I slowed my breathing, focused my mind, stilled my emotions.

Everything around me slowed, too. I closed my eyes and let images of Goku's dead body fall out of my mind like leaves from a tree.

And then I heard Ken-ichi advancing toward me, feet crunching the sand, sword whistling as it was raised to strike. I opened my eyes and brought my blade up and defended easily. As he gathered himself for another backhanded slice, I used the force of his attack to propel my sword around into an attack on him, forcing him to turn his strike into a block.

He was off balance for a moment and I saw my opportunity. I spun, twisting my hips and snapping my foot forward to kick him. I heard my foot connect with his chest, and he staggered.

Ken-ichi's mouth opened wide in shock and I knew he was shouting something, but I couldn't hear. My ears were filled with the sweet sigh of the warm spring air. I felt a huge energy pulsing inside me and I channeled it all into my right foot as I unleashed the same *yokogeri* kick that had felled the willow tree.

This is for Goku! I thought triumphantly.

But sound came crashing back in as Ken-ichi stepped to the side and snatched at my right foot. He trapped it beneath his arm, hard, and I had a sudden memory of the way he had injured the young student in training a few days ago. With a triumphant sneer and a chuckle, Ken-ichi twisted, and I knew that this time he wouldn't hold back. He would break my ankle.

I went with the motion. I let him twist, but I twisted too, using the strength in my cousin's grip to spin my body in midair. My other foot came up and for a moment I was flying. Time stood still as I spun horizontally through the air, channeling all the power in my body through my left leg. I felt a jolt as my heel connected with Ken-ichi's chin.

He staggered, pain etched across his face. His arm loosened and suddenly my right foot was free. I landed lightly on my feet, my back to him.

My kick had stunned him. His feet were planted wide. His sword dangled limply at his side.

I didn't hesitate. I launched myself forward into another *yokogeri* kick. My foot slammed into Ken-ichi's chest and he went flying backward, face amazed. He went flying through one section of the crowd, which parted like a hastily raised curtain, and slammed into the wall of the courtyard.

He was motionless for a moment, looking breathless, like a butterfly that had been pinned. Then slowly he slid down the wall into a crumpled heap.

Around me, men and women in colorful kimonos surged upward and suddenly everyone stood, roaring and applauding. But I couldn't think about them now. All I could see was the sword in Ken-ichi's hand.

I strode toward him and stepped on the blade, pinning it to the ground and aiming the point of my sword at his throat.

"It is over now," I said, and my voice sounded loud in the hush that fell on the courtyard. "Yield!"

CHAPTER TWENTY-TWO

Ken-ichi looked up at me. For a moment I could see a look of surprise flash across his face. I realized that he had expected me to kill him.

He was still breathless and there was a tiny trickle of blood beneath one of his nostrils. He shook his head, refusing to accept that he had lost.

"Yield, Ken-ichi," I said in a gentle voice. "You've been defeated."

"That's what you think, rice boy," Ken-ichi growled. "A Yamamoto is never beaten."

I know that, I wanted to say. *Because I am a Yamamoto through and through. And after everything I have been through, I am still not beaten.*

But I knew that now wasn't the right time to tell Ken-ichi who I was.

I took my foot off his sword. "Get up," I said.

He stared at me for a moment; then he scrambled to his feet, re-sheathing his sword in one movement.

"You may have beaten me in this fight, rice boy," he said. "But you haven't won anything. I'm still the son of the *Jito*. And you're still nothing more than a filthy peasant."

With that, he abruptly turned and ran away across the courtyard. For a moment he was silhouetted in the gateway, and then he was gone.

"Ken-ichi!" I yelled, and I would have gone after him but Hana appeared at my side.

She took my hand in hers, her grip surprisingly strong. "Let him go," she said. "He has to run away."

"Why?" I asked

She gazed at me, her eyes clear pools of light. "If he stays, he would be dragged in front of the *Jito* to stand trial for his treachery," she said simply. "He's a murderer now. And a murderer cannot expect mercy, even if he is the son of the *Jito*."

She was still gazing at me when the crowd suddenly surged forward and surrounded us. People reached out to thump me on the back. "What a victory!" someone cried. "The Master is avenged!"

But I felt no sense of satisfaction. I didn't want revenge for Master Goku's death—I wanted the Master alive and well, standing at my side. My heart ached as I thought of the deaths I had seen since that afternoon when Uncle had arrived at our compound—Father, Harumasa, Nobuaki, all our faithful servants, and now Sensei, too.

I walked through the crowd to kneel once more at Master Goku's side. Choji, Tatsuya, and Ko were kneeling beside him, their heads bowed in prayer.

Choji stood up as I approached, and placed a hand on my shoulder. I swallowed hard, but it was no good. I could not hold back the tears.

Tatsuya got to his feet. "Goku-sensei was like a father to me, and Ken-ichi murdered him," he said in a bitter voice. "I am not sure he deserved the mercy you showed him in letting him go."

"Goku-san was like a father to me, too," I murmured. "We have each lost two fathers, Tatsuya—our own and Sensei."

Choji squeezed my shoulder once with his powerful hand, and then he patted Tatsuya on the back in a comforting way before turning to speak to the crowd. "The tournament must be suspended," he said, spreading his arms wide to encompass everyone present. "I beg all of you to accept our apologies. Return to your homes. Leave us to mourn, and to prepare for the funeral of our Master."

Merchants and craftsmen shuffled and murmured. Choji gave a few instructions and people began to move away from the fight arena. Some of them came forward to bow respectfully to Master Goku's body.

Hana was still kneeling at Goku's side. I put my arm lightly around her shoulders. The touch of my hand on her shoulder seemed to release a wave of emotion. She began to cry, tears rolling down her cheeks to wet the sandy floor. There was nothing I could say to comfort her, so I simply held her for a moment. A few men and women glanced curiously at us.

Tatsuya touched my arm. "Why don't you both go inside?" he suggested. "You can get away from the crowds."

I looked at Hana, and she nodded. Tatsuya helped us both to our feet. "I'll stay and help move Master Goku," he said quietly.

A few samurai came to stand in a row nearby, hands on the hilts of their swords, as if forming a guard of honor to escort the Master to his resting place.

Hana and I began to make our way across the arena, weaving through the crowd. All at once, she stopped in her tracks and stared at the cherry blossom trees on the other side of the courtyard.

"What's the matter?" I asked.

"Beneath the cherry blossom trees," she murmured, her voice so quiet I could barely hear her. "What did he mean, Kimi? *Beneath the cherry blossoms . . .*"

"I don't know," I said.

"I want to look over there."

"We can't," I said, glancing around at all the people. A few of them had gone, but most were still milling around, talking quietly as they packed up their belongings. "Not now, Hana. But we can come back later tonight, when everyone's gone."

Her gaze still seemed drawn to the trees. A breeze stirred the branches and more blossoms fell softly to the ground. But at last she nodded and let me lead her away through the gardens. Gravel crunched beneath our feet. The sounds from the courtyard grew more and more faint.

As we passed the meditation room, Hana hesitated. A frown creased her brow. Abruptly she pulled away from me and hurried up the steps. She kicked off her shoes and entered silently.

I followed her inside, expecting Hana to kneel and perhaps meditate. But her stride didn't hesitate. She made her way across the room to the opposite wall, where she stopped and gazed at a long scroll hanging on a red silk ribbon.

I caught my breath.

The scroll was covered in elegant brushstrokes. Beautiful thick lines swept upward, curved out, and then fluttered in a series of tiny white paint flecks . . . the perfect depiction of a cherry tree in blossom.

"'Beneath the cherry blossoms,'" Hana said in a

soft, breathless voice, and she reached sideways to hold my hand as we both looked down.

Below the scroll was a low lacquered table. The front was screened with a blue silk curtain.

I kneeled down and drew aside the curtain. Under the table was a cedarwood casket. My hands trembled as I lifted the casket and set it on top of the table. I glanced up at Hana, a question in my eyes.

She nodded. "Open it," she whispered.

Carefully I lifted the lid.

A breath of perfumed air seemed to puff out, carrying the scent of cherry blossoms. Peering inside the casket, I saw seven tiny scrolls, each with a broken wax seal and a scarlet ribbon.

I took out the first one and carefully unfurled it. "Oh, Hana!" I murmured, immediately recognizing the elegant brushstrokes and perfect *kanji*. "It's a letter from Mother."

> *Dearest Goku,*
> *How glad I was to receive your news that my daughters are in your custody. I know that you will keep them safe from harm, and that their well-being is one worry that I can let go of. . . .*

My mother's writing blurred as tears sprang to my eyes. I could almost hear her voice, saying the words.

"Mother has reached the town," I said to Hana,

quickly reading the rest of the letter. "She is staying with an old friend of Father's."

Hana reached sideways and gripped my arm. "And Moriyasu?"

I scanned the scroll. "He's well," I said, relief making me light-headed. "She says he asks for news of us every day, and she's glad that she can now tell him where we are."

My hands moved among the other three scrolls, hastily unrolling each one, scanning, and moving on to the next. "She and Goku have been corresponding for the past few weeks," I said. "But she doesn't say where they are."

"We will find them," Hana said, clutching one of the letters in her hand. She took a deep breath, and I could see the resolve on her face. "Our time here at the dojo has given us strength and purpose. Master Goku may not be here, Kimi, but we will carry him with us in our talents and sword skills."

I put the letters back into the box and embraced my sister. "Together, we can do anything."

As we held each other, Hana continued, "We will search for Mother and Moriyasu . . . and we will find them. And one day, we will avenge Father and Harumasa and Nobuaki, and the honor of the Yamamoto family will be restored."

Our journey had only just begun.

EPILOGUE

I can move as silently as a ghost, a *kami* spirit walking the earth. I can make my way through a grand celebration at the Shogun's court, rubbing shoulders with nobles and lords.

But they will pass me by, never knowing I am there.

When I move past a shrine in a forest, the few who stand to silently pray do not see me at all.

I walk alone along the waters of the eastern sea, where only the sunset watches me.

Almost alone, but not quite.

Because those who have died on my path walk with me every step.

That day, kneeling in the meditation room with Hana at my side, I knew it was time to leave the safety of the dojo and follow a new path.

I knew that one day my softly treading foot-steps would carry me forward to meet Mother and Moriyasu. . . .

And I hoped that my courage would allow me to

restore the honor of my family. My heart was filled with hope that, once we were together, I would be able to keep them safe.

How could I have known what tragedies awaited us?

Kimi and Hana's adventures
continue in

Sisters of the Sword

CHASING THE SECRET

Turn the page for a sneak peek!

CHAPTER ONE

It was shortly after dawn, and my sister, Hana, and I were in our small room in the servants' quarter of our samurai-training school.

A fresh early-morning breeze blew in through an open bamboo screen, bringing with it the scent of cherry blossom petals crushed by the overnight rain. Outside, the sky was slowly lightening, and droplets of water sparkled on the leaves and flowers in the garden.

Hana and I kneeled opposite each other, our hands resting lightly on our thighs. We were dressed in our usual servants' outfits of a short blue jacket, blue breeches, and bare feet. We had been meditating quietly, but now it was time to face the day ahead. Tonight would be very hard.

"Master Goku's funeral . . . ," Hana murmured. Her voice sounded tight, as if she was close to tears. "I don't think I can bear it, Kimi."

I reached out and smoothed her long hair, hanging loose over her shoulder like silky black rope. "We have to bear it," I said gently. "Master Goku is dead, and there is nothing we can do to change that."

"I wish Mother were here," Hana whispered.

"I wish that, too," I said.

An image of Mother as I had last seen her blazed across my mind. It was dusk, and she had been sitting with Father and Uncle in the rock garden. As Hana and I had led away our brother Moriyasu to his bedchambers, I'd glanced back over my shoulder and seen Mother smiling at Father. Her face had been so serene and confident, full of strength and wisdom.

My heart twisted at the thought of how happy we had been then. Before my uncle had ripped us apart.

Would I ever see Mother again? My soul lifted with the hope that one day Mother, Moriyasu, Hana, and I could be together forever. I thought of the bamboo sword hiding in our storage basket, my little brother's favorite toy, and renewed my vow to return it to him.

I dragged my thoughts back to the present. "One day at a time," I said firmly, more to myself than Hana. "We just need to get through tonight. Mother's letter will soon arrive, telling us where to meet her."

2

Before he took his last breath, Master Goku told us of his cedarwood box full of our mother's letters. A true friend, he had risked everything to arrange for our reunion. Mother had said she would send one more instruction to tell us how to find her.

One final letter. One more precious paper scroll.

"Then we can go to her," Hana said, "and be a family again. . . ."

The sound of hurrying feet came from the hallway outside.

"Everybody up!" came the deep, rumbling voice of Mr. Choji, the head servant. Since Master Goku's death, Choji had taken over the dojo and now everyone addressed him more respectfully as Mr. Choji.

Hana and I exchanged a horrified glance. If Mr. Choji came into our room now, he would see our long hair tumbling over our shoulders and know in an instant that we were girls.

"We're coming," I called out as we leaped to our feet, scrambling to twist up our hair into boyish topknots.

"I need you all, right away." Mr. Choji seemed in a panic. "The *Jito* is coming and he wants the funeral to take place immediately!"

The *Jito*? The blood in my veins pulsed furiously. Mr. Choji meant Lord Hidehira, our uncle. The man who had murdered our father and brothers. And

3

now he was disrupting the arrangements for the funeral of our murdered Master. The thought made anger fill my heart like black smoke. How dare he? When his own son had been responsible for Master Goku's death!

I paused at the door, and turned back to see Hana's shaking hands quickly secure her hair with a pointed, metal hairpin. I raised my eyebrows to ask if she was ready, and when she nodded I slid back the bamboo screen and came face-to-face with Mr. Choji.

He was a gruff, good-natured man, round faced and stocky, with black hair that he wore pulled into the traditional samurai's oiled tail, tightly folded on the top of his head. On our arrival, Mr. Choji had taken Hana and me under his wing, affectionately calling us "skinny boys" as he fed us hearty meals of soup and noodles.

"Quickly, boys! We are not prepared for the *Jito*," Mr. Choji said. "I need one of you to ring the bell and wake the students, while the other goes to the kitchens and brings out the ceremonial tea bowls." He clapped his hands and turned away in a flurry of pale gray kimono robes. "Hurry!"

"I'll ring the bell," I said to my sister.

Hana nodded. "I will prepare the tea bowls and meet you in the kitchens afterward."

4

We dashed after Mr. Choji, who was striding along the narrow hallway. He knocked on wooden door frames as he went, calling out to the sleeping occupants. Screen doors slid back, revealing yawning boys in breeches with tousled hair.

"What's happening?" someone asked. "Are we under attack?"

"Get up! Get dressed!" Mr. Choji cried, clapping his hands. "We've just had word that the *Jito* is coming—the funeral will be this morning."

"The *Jito* is coming. . . ." The urgent whisper carried along the hallway, traveling from one room to the next. "This morning?" servants asked in confusion. Master Goku's body was to be moved this evening to the temple, and the funeral wasn't supposed to take place until tonight.

Through an open doorway I caught a glimpse of my friend Ko rubbing his eyes, and then Hana and I were outside, thrusting our feet into our sandals and racing along the covered walkway that led to the gardens. Hana headed for the kitchens, the soles of her sandals flashing as she hurried. I turned and ran along gravel pathways that led through the dojo gardens, ducking beneath overhanging branches.

As I reached the bell tower I saw the sun rising, a bright crimson ball painting the sky pink and orange. I ran up the bell tower steps and hauled on

5

the rope to swing the wooden beam against the metal. The beam was heavy and it took two strong tugs to get it swinging. At last the deep, sonorous sound rang out, echoing across the gardens and reverberating against the far walls of the dojo.

I kept pulling, ringing the bell again and again.

From my vantage point I could see the dojo laid out beneath me: Neatly swept pathways cut through green moss gardens; pools of still water reflected the early-morning sky; curving red rooftops rose up from the foliage like the wings of exotic birds. Trees clung to the hillside behind the dojo, interrupted only by the long path that led up to the temple.

This place had become home, a haven from the man that hunted us. But now with Goku gone, I didn't know if we could remain safe here.

Stilling the rope, I watched as screen doors flew back in the students' quarters. Boys of all ages hurried onto the walkways, some still tying up their hair while they ran to their duties. Others looked as if they had been up for hours, meditating or practicing their kata movements. Junior masters in black robes quickly joined them.

Everyone was awake now, and the dojo took on an air of bustling purpose. As I headed back toward the kitchens, I realized that someone had fallen into step beside me.

"I've heard the news," a voice said. I glanced up into the concerned face of my friend Tatsuya, the only person other than Master Goku that Hana and I had trusted with our secret. He was dressed formally for the funeral, his short white kimono jacket neatly pressed and the soft fabric of his black *hakama* trousers pooling around his feet. A long curved sword in its scabbard was tucked into his sash.

"Where's Hana?" he asked as he limped slightly with every other step. His ankle was still hurting him after Ken-ichi, Uncle's son, sabotaged him at the tournament, but it was healing quickly.

"She's in the kitchens," I replied, "preparing for the Kaminari's arrival." Kaminari, meaning "thunder," was the nickname the people had given to Uncle because he raged through their villages like a storm.

"I won't let anything happen to either of you," Tatsuya said.

I paused at the end of the walkway and bowed to him. "Thank you, Tatsuya." It was good to know we had a friend.

"Do you think Hidehira is coming here to look for Ken-ichi?" Tatsuya asked as we walked on.

"Maybe," I replied. Then another thought made me shudder. "Or maybe someone has seen through our disguise and he is coming here to find us."

Tatsuya shook his head. "No, he can't have discovered you. Just try to stay out of his way."

We walked over a low wooden footbridge and came to a fork in the path. Several students were gathered there, listening to one of the junior masters give them hurried instructions for the rescheduled funeral. Their faces were somber.

"I should go," I said. "Mr. Choji will need my help."

Tatsuya nodded and I hurried away to join Hana in the kitchens. I found her laying out tea bowls on a lacquered tray. Mr. Choji caught sight of me and gestured impatiently. "Skinny boy, come with me. And bring your brother. It is almost time for me to go to the main courtyard and receive Lord Hidehira. You will attend me."

My thoughts began to race. Attending Mr. Choji meant standing close while he greeted Uncle. Close enough for Uncle to recognize us if he looked closely. We would have to be careful not to draw attention to ourselves. Hana looked anxious. We both knew that if Uncle realized who we were, all would be lost.

"Don't just stand there, skinny boys," Mr. Choji cried, turning and heading for the door in a flurry of gray robes. "Follow me."

We leaped to obey, following Mr. Choji out of the kitchens and along the walkways. The last few students were streaming toward the archway leading to the main courtyard, their black *hakama* trousers fluttering as they ran.

As we passed one of the moss gardens, Mr. Choji slowed his step to allow Hana and me to catch up. "You seem surprised that I have chosen you to attend me this morning," he said as we walked beside him. "Master Goku thought highly of you, so it is fitting for you both to stand behind me as I greet His Lordship formally in the courtyard. Afterward we will proceed to the pavilion in the moss garden for the *cha no yoriai* tea ceremony. Is that understood?"

"Yes, Mr. Choji," we murmured. A memory flashed in my mind. The last time I had been in that pavilion, I had almost assassinated my uncle. Master Goku had stopped me and taught me the only honorable way to avenge my father was to challenge Uncle openly.

Running footsteps crunched the gravel on the pathway behind us and we quickly moved aside to let two of the younger students past.

"Hurry now," Mr. Choji called to them. "Don't be late."

"Yes, Mr. Choji," the boys said, bowing quickly before they raced on toward the main courtyard.

Mr. Choji watched them go and then turned back

to Hana and me.

"Today will be a difficult day for the students," he said. "It's almost unbearable to think that we will be saying good-bye to Master Goku for the last time."

I bowed my head, suddenly so full of grief that I could not trust myself to speak.

"This situation will be awkward for Lord Hidehira, too," Mr. Choji went on. I thought I caught a note of disapproval in his voice when he said Uncle's name. "Long ago, Lord Hidehira attended this school. With Ken-ichi responsible for Goku's death, the Lord Steward will feel the pain of Goku's death twice over—the loss of his Master and the disgrace of his son."

"Yes, Mr. Choji," I said again. But privately I did not think Uncle was the sort of man to feel pain or loss. He had killed his own brother! He had no feelings. Nothing but his desire for power mattered to him.

We came to the wooden archway that led into the sandy main courtyard. Two guards in leather armor stood on either side of the front gate, their iron helmets gleaming.

Mr. Choji paused for a moment, closing his eyes and stilling himself. Then he gave Hana and me a nod as we stepped through the archway.

Before us were row upon row of seated students.

10

There were about a hundred students and teachers gathered all together. Although they were trying to be quiet and respectful as they awaited the arrival of the *Jito*, the wide open space seemed to pulse with their energy and anticipation. The tallest students stood at the back against the rear wall of the courtyard, their black belts showing their seniority. The younger ones kneeled in the formal *seiza* position at the front, their hands resting lightly on their knees.

Mr. Choji made his way to the center of the courtyard, ready to welcome our important visitor. Hana and I hurried to stand behind him, our heads bowed. A hush descended. The only sounds were the breeze whispering through the pine trees surrounding the dojo and the gentle splash of a waterfall in one of the gardens nearby.

A conch-shell horn sounded, signaling the approach of the *Jito*. As the sound faded away, the muffled thunder of horses' hooves rose in the still morning air.

I glanced at Hana. Her face was composed but pale. I tried taking a deep breath to calm myself, but inside I was in turmoil at the thought of seeing Uncle Hidehira once more.

The thundering hooves came closer. I opened my eyes as more than ten mounted samurai galloped in through the open gates, their red silk *mon* badges gleaming at their shoulders. Glittering swords were strapped to their waists and quivers of arrows bristled at their backs.

The samurai's horses churned up the carefully swept sand as they wheeled and spread out to line the walls on either side of the courtyard. Through the gates behind them came an ornate black-lacquered palanquin carried on the shoulders of four bearers in scarlet livery, its white silk curtains rippling in the breeze.

The sight of this palanquin used to thrill me with anticipation of my father's appearance, but now, knowing the evil man who would emerge, all I felt was disgust.

The palanquin came to a halt in the center of the courtyard just as more samurai on horseback came cantering in through the gates. Their captain gave a curt order and the two guards hurried to close the gates behind them.

The bearers set the palanquin down and my body tensed. Beside me, Hana stood as still as a marble statue, her gaze fixed to the ground in front of her.

A large, powerful hand appeared at the curtains, crushing the fragile silk. The curtains were roughly pulled aside and Uncle Hidehira appeared. His thin-lipped smile didn't reach his dark eyes. Loathing filled my soul.

Mr. Choji made a gesture, and as one, the school bowed. Hana and I placed our hands on our thighs and bent low.

As we rose, Uncle Hidehira stepped down from the palanquin. He straightened up, hands on hips, his broad shoulders dwarfing the guards who stood on each side. He surveyed the assembled school. His gaze seemed to penetrate deep into the soul of each person he looked at.

I kept my head bowed but peeked at Uncle from beneath my eyelashes, studying him carefully. Father always said, *Know your opponent as well as you know yourself because that is how you will discover his weakness.*

Usually Uncle wore robes of glossy red silk to signify his important role as *Jito,* but now he was dressed traditionally in white for the funeral. The many layers of his luxurious kimono moved heavily as he walked across the courtyard toward Mr. Choji. His black hair had been shaved at the front, then oiled and folded in an ornate ceremonial style. Two swords—one long, one slightly shorter—were stuck into his stiffened obi sash.

Uncle returned Mr. Choji's respectful bow, but his own bow was slight, and I guessed that he felt it was beneath him to show a mere head servant too much honor.

The two men greeted each other formally in low

voices. I could see tension on my uncle's face. His confident air was betrayed by the new lines on his forehead. Perhaps it was us, the surviving witnesses of his treachery, that weighed on his mind. I hoped it was.

A sharp thought filled my mind: I had an advantage over Uncle. Despite all his power, I knew something he didn't. My mother and brother were alive and safe—and soon we would be together again. I was sure of it.

Hana shifted beside me and I reached out to her, touching her fingers in our secret signal of kinship.

Mr. Choji bowed to Uncle Hidehira once more, robes rippling. "Will you do me the honor of accepting a bowl of tea in our pavilion, Lord Hidehira?"

Uncle Hidehira gazed at him for a moment, his eyes as black and expressionless as a lizard's. "No tea, thank you."

My heart began to pump harder. By refusing tea, Uncle was dishonoring Mr. Choji in front of the whole school.

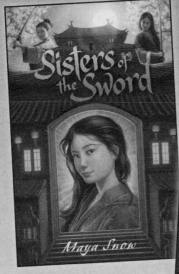